HIGH
WATER

HIGH WATER

By Megan Tolley

and

Diane Stringam Tolley

Summary: A flood in Banff National Park creates magical mayhem among the long-preserved animals in the museum.

ISBN-13: **978-1518708091**

ISBN-10: **1518708099**

Cover design © 2015 by Diane Tolley

Edited by Caitlin Clark

Dedication

To everyone who has ever wished for a bear (or a moose or an elk or a skunk or a wolf or an eagle, etc.) as a pet.

Prologue

Michael stood by the big east window and stared forlornly out in the direction of the Bow River. Heavy rain beat against the thick glass, making it difficult to see exactly what was going on, but he could almost feel the slow creep of the muddy water as it grew closer and closer to his beloved Banff Park Museum. He could certainly hear the great roar of the Bow Falls such a short distance downstream.

He sighed, his thoughts turning to the vast collection of over 5000 birds, animals and insects so carefully displayed and stored in the old building. Many of them dated back to the 1893 World Exhibition in Chicago!

Water, even a small amount, would destroy them completely.

Michael looked around. What would Norman Sanson, the museum's last curator, have done? He wondered, then shook his head. He knew what Mr. Sanson would have done. Something proactive and amazing. Hadn't he, by the year 1932, been largely responsible for completing the collecting of the greater part of the birds, animals, fish, reptiles and insects stored here?

Michael spun around as someone burst in through the front doors. Two figures in yellow rain gear. One of them slid his heavy hood back and removed dripping goggles. "Sorry, Mac," he said. "The river's rising even faster now. The Trans-Canada bridge has washed out in Canmore. We have to get you out now before you're completely cut off!"

"But Canmore's twelve miles away . . .!" Michael began. He turned back to the window and tried once more to see out. Then he looked at the birds and animals all around him and finally, up at the mounted elk and cougar standing high above on one of the main cabinets. "If the water reaches here, they will be ruined," he said in a small voice. "Most of them are . . . irreplaceable."

The man in the yellow coat shrugged his shoulders. "Nothing we can do about them, Mac," he said. "They're dead. Our concern is the living. You."

Michael sighed and nodded. "I know," he said, sadly. "I'll get my things." He disappeared down into his office in the basement.

The two men remained by the front door, their wet coats streaming water onto the mat.

One of them looked around. "It is a shame," he said. "It really is quite a priceless collection."

The other man nodded. "But if it comes to a decision between them or their care-taker, our choice is easy."

The second man nodded. "I know."

Just then, Michael appeared at the top of the stairs, carrying a heavy briefcase and a long coat. He set the case on the floor and pulled on his coat. He then picked up his case and, shutting the basement door, crossed the room. "I'm ready," he said, quietly. "As ready as I'll ever be," he added under his breath.

"Good," the first man said. "Let's go!" The two of them pushed open the big doors and stepped out into the pouring rain.

Michael followed, snapping off lights, setting the alarm system and, last of all, pulling the doors carefully shut behind him. He locked them, staring for a moment at the lock, then at the heavy key in his hand. Finally he shrugged. "Habit," he said, mostly to himself.

Pocketing the key, he grasped the handle of his briefcase and nodded to his two rescuers. "Whenever you're ready," he said.

Each of them grabbed one of his arms and hustled him out into the downpour.

* * *

For several minutes the old log building sat, silent. The only sound was the drumming of water from the heavy rain, the only light, from the interior security system and the occasional flashes of lightning. Occasionally, the old roof would creak slightly against a sudden gust of wind. But the heavy logs used when it was constructed in 1903 didn't even quiver in the onslaught.

Outside, the river crept steadily closer.

Higher.

It lapped against the outside wall, then swirled higher still, slipping around the corners and swirling against some of the lower windows.

At that moment, the power suddenly went out and, for a moment, inky blackness descended. From somewhere, something snorted. Then came the sound of fluttering wings. The stamp of a hoof. Then the battery-powered emergency lights flashed on, casting light on a strange scene below.

The bald eagle atop the main cabinet lowered its wings and looked around, great eyes peering in the gloom. The elk standing beside it lowered its head slowly. Both turned as the cougar and the bear, so long their companions on the high perch, suddenly made their way down from the cabinet. The big cat leaping smoothly, its great paws landing soundlessly on the linoleum and the bear following more cautiously, backwards. Then the great cat, instinctively heading for higher ground, made its way quickly to the upper stairway and started up, the bear close behind.

All around them, the birds, animals and insects awoke. Wings long dormant flapped and shook. Eyes blinked. Heads turned.

A steady stream of bugs and insects gathered at the edge of their cabinets, looking for a way down.

At that point, the elk swung his great head and studied the floor far below. Then he snorted and leaped. Just as his hooves thumped down, the glass beside him shattered and the family of bison and one coyote, for so many years his neighbours in the next case, charged through, nearly colliding with him.

The animals scrambled slightly for footing on the unaccustomed slick surface.

Then the elk turned to look toward the stairway.

The bull bison followed his gaze and nodded, then herded his family toward higher ground. As he passed the insect display cabinets, the great bull paused a moment to allow them to stream onto his back, then proceeded up the stairs, his mate and calf following.

The great wolves that had stood for years atop the bison cabinet leapt lightly to the floor and trailed behind in single file.

At that moment, the door to the basement burst open and animals surged out. They paused for only a moment, then turning, followed their friends toward the upper stairway.

The great elk, antlers gleaming in the scanty light, began to move from cabinet to cabinet, swinging his heavy headgear and smashing the cabinet glass that kept the smaller birds and animals captive. The birds, flapping long-unused wings, headed immediately for the upper reaches while many of the smaller animals streamed across the floor to reach the comparative safety of the staircase.

Larger animals stopped to help those too small to risk the short trip in the gloom. Two gophers were busily pulling the pins that impaled some of the insects and dropping them heedlessly. A family of mice rode in comfort on the back of the loon as it waddled placidly across the floor.

As the large bird passed the main cabinet, the big-horned ram, long encased there as a centerpiece, burst through the heavy glass. Followed quickly by the rest of its tiny herd of sheep and goats, the animal followed the loon.

Slowly, the migration to the stairway increased.

If any animals appeared confused, the elk quickly moved to their side and indicated the way with a twitch of his head. As he passed the display of preserved birds' eggs, the great animal turned to note the cracking and splintering of all of the delicate globes. The peeping and chittering of the newly-hatched. Moving closer, the elk carefully broke the glass in one corner, then stood quietly as the tiny babies, flightless still, made their way clumsily but efficiently through the opening and onto his tall back.

Then, moving carefully, he climbed up the stairs and deposited his cargo on one of the old, oak tables.

He made a circuit of the upper cases, smashing glass and freeing animals. As he approached the two bears, first one, then the other, casually swatted with great paws at the offending glass imprisoning them and lumbered out onto the floor.

All watched as a great trout, floating gently in midair, swam lazily past.

Turning, the elk made his way back down the staircase and began to search through the lower floor for stragglers.

Finally, he again made his way up the now-crowded stairs and took up a position overlooking the lower gallery.

The fluttering and shuffling quietened as the animals settled.

Finally, all was still once more.

Only the sound of the rain drumming on the roof remained.

* * *

"Well, let me tell you, it was a long four days!" Michael said as he stopped in front of the doors. For a moment, he looked toward the river, noted the debris left by the receding water. Then he turned to stare at the water marks on the doors and walls. He sighed.

"Well, there's undoubtedly a lot of damage," his companion said. "Even though the Rangers don't think any water got through."

Michael put his key into the door. "I know." He sounded hopeful. "But they never checked out the basement . . . Well, come on Ben, let's get this over with." He turned the lock and pulled.

The door opened, but with difficulty, squeaking loudly on its hinges.

Michael stepped inside and shook his head. Apart from a more-than-damp front area carpet, the floor looked untouched. Then he moved further inside and noticed . . . glass. Broken pieces and shards of it were everywhere.

He looked up and frowned. Strange. For a moment, in the weak light, it looked as though the cabinets. . .

"Michael," his companion whispered. "The glass is broken! The cases are all empty!"

Michael blinked and rubbed his eyes. They were. He spun around. The glass from every case had been smashed out. The animals and birds were gone.

All of them.

He felt faint. "Who could have possibly . . .?"

"Someone must have broken in and . . ."

Just then, both of them heard a noise. Something was moving on the second floor. They looked up.

The eyes of hundreds of birds and animals glowed palely in the light from the 'lantern' windows as they looked down over the upper bannister at the two men.

"What . . .?" Michael whispered.

This time he did faint.

* * *

"What do you mean the displays in the museum have suddenly come to life?" Ms. Kennard wasn't impressed. She had been working since dawn, trying to sort out the outside damage and needed repairs. She put her clipboard under one arm and clicked her pen.

[6]

Michael felt his face redden, but he stood his ground. "That's exactly what's happened," he said, firmly. "Every animal, bird, bug, insect, egg. Everything in that building."

"I don't believe you," Ms. Kennard said bluntly. She narrowed her eyes. "Have you been drinking?"

Michael shook his head and ran a hand through his short, brown hair. "Ms. Kennard, you'll just have to come with me and see for yourself."

She frowned and sighed. "Very well, Michael. Let's get this farce over with." She followed him out of the building and up the street.

"I'll warn you, it's a bit startling."

"Are you here about the crazy story, too, Susan?" someone asked.

Both of them spun around.

Ben was approaching with a third man. Ben's eyes met Michael's and the two of them nodded.

"Well, Jacob, if Benjamin told you the same story that Michael told me, then yes," Ms. Kennard said. She shrugged. "I guess there's only one way to prove it!" she put her hand on the doorknob.

"Careful!" Michael said.

Ms. Kennard snorted and pulled. The door creaked open.

All of them heard the distinct fluttering of wings as they stepped inside.

All four of them looked up and Ms. Kennard gasped.

The great bald eagle was perched on the bannister, its wings spread and glowing in the early morning light. As they watched, it launched itself into the air and spinning in a tight circle, landed directly in front of them. Its beak opened and it let out a loud screech. Then it tipped its head and stared at them, unblinking.

"I guess you're telling the truth," Ms. Kennard said, her voice faint. "I think I need to . . ." she sank into a nearby chair.

Jacob shook his head. "I don't believe it."

Michael lifted a hand, directing them all to look up.

Birds and animals were peering over the bannister at them. As they watched, the great elk who had once stood atop the largest display case in the center of the room slowly began to descend the stairs.

"Careful," Michael said. "We don't know how it's going to react and it *is* a wild animal."

As the elk continued to move toward them, the four humans took shelter inside the tiny admissions kiosk. Finally, the animal stopped a short distance away and looked at them.

They stared back.

It turned its great head and surveyed the other animals and birds, many of which were beginning to come down the stairs or fly to the tops of the lower floor cabinets.

Michael stared at the great beast for a moment, then suddenly thrust out his hand.

"Careful!" Ms. Kennard said.

The elk moved closer and touched the extended hand with a soft nose.

"Huh," Michael said.

"What?"

"It's warm!"

"Then it truly *is* alive!" Ms. Kennard said softly.

Michael nodded, not taking his eyes from the huge animal. "I think we're going to have to change our signs," he whispered. "The Banff Park Museum has just become the Banff Park Zoo!"

Chapter One

Thirteen-year-old Avery had been sitting on the couch for an hour, waiting impatiently for her father to come home. She had tried to read the new novel about shape-shifting humans that she had just brought home from the library, but couldn't seem to focus.

Finally, his car pulled into the driveway.

She leaped to her feet and ran to the door, pulling it open just as he reached it. "Is it true?" she asked breathlessly.

"Why, hello honey!" her dad said, tiredly. "I had a good day, thanks for asking, and I'm very happy to be home in the bosom of my family once more."

Avery made a face and gave her father a quick hug. Then, "Is it true?" she asked again, stepping back and staring at him intently.

"Is what true?" he asked, handing her his heavy briefcase and stopping to remove his wet and muddy shoes.

"You know what!" Avery said, carrying his briefcase to the closet and setting it down. "The thing you told Mom this afternoon!"

Just then, Avery's mom came into the entry. "Hello, Michael," she said, giving her husband a hug. She smoothed his hair. "Nice day?"

Her dad sighed. "Weird day. The only practical thing we managed to do was ascertain the damage to the building."

"Was there much damage?" Avery's mom asked, her face suddenly pinched with concern.

"Surprisingly little," he said. "The new concrete held up well and the stones did what stones do in a foundation. The files are safe and all of the animals are . . . well, I guess you know."

She nodded.

"Grrrrrr! Tellmetellmetellmetellmetellme!" Avery said, jumping up and down.

Her mom smiled. "She hasn't let up since you called to give us the news."

Avery's dad smiled. "Well, it is rather . . . exciting news."

"Exciting! Dad! Hundred-year-old mounted animals that have been on display for over a century suddenly come to life?" Avery shook her head. "This isn't just exciting! It's . . . stupendous! It's mind-blowing! It's earth-shattering! It's . . .!"

"I think we get the point, honey," her mother said, soothingly.

"So when can I see them?!" Avery reached for her father's hand and shook it up and down. "When? Whenwhenwhenwhenwhenwhenwhen?"

"Oh, I don't think . . ." her father began.

"Da-ad!" Avery said, shuffling from foot to foot. "You have to be kidding! This is the chance of a lifetime! Don't tell me I can't see them!"

"Well, there is the ongoing clean up in the townsite and . . ."

"I'll avoid the puddles," Avery said.

"There's a lot more than 'puddles'," her dad said. "They're calling it the worst storm in over a hundred years and it did a lot of damage."

"Well, I'm old enough to know how to stay away from anything dangerous!"

"Those *animals* could be dangerous," her dad said. "They are – or were – wild."

"I'll be careful," Avery said. "I'll only look in the window."

Her dad smiled. "I'm afraid you wouldn't see much," he said. "We've shut everything up tight, trying to rein in the curiosity seekers until we can get things sorted out."

"But Dad, I want to see them!" Avery looked at her father, her eyes pleading. She had never wanted anything more in her life.

"It's too dangerous, honey," her dad said, rubbing one hand over his head. "They are too unpredictable at this point." He shrugged. "We locked up the museum and shuttered the windows." He made a face. "Still, it took about five minutes for the rumor mill to start up. I don't know how these things leak out, but they certainly do."

"You have to admit that it's quite a story," her mom said.

Her dad looked at her mom and snorted softly. "Quite a story indeed, Maureen. Thousands of mounted animals, many of them older than the park itself, suddenly brought to life!"

Her mom raised her eyebrows. "Have the powers-that-be got any ideas about what occurred?"

"None," her dad said. "They're . . . absolutely stumped!"

"I can tell you what happened," Avery said.

Both of her parents looked at her. Avery was thirteen and tall, with her mom's long, blonde hair and her dad's clear, blue eyes. She was a top student, especially in Science. It wouldn't be the first time she figured something out before they did.

"What do you think happened?" her dad asked.

"I think that the water was magic," Avery said.

"Magic? That's your explanation?" her dad rolled his eyes.

"Hear her out, dear," her mom said quietly.

Her dad sighed. "Go on, honey," he said.

"Yup. I think that there was so much water that it washed through places in the mountains it had never touched before. You said yourself that it was the worst storm in over a hundred years. What if it ran across some of the Ktunaxa, Salish or Stoney people's Sacred Ground?"

[11]

Her dad stared at his daughter. "Sacred Ground?"

"Dad, with all of the native peoples moving through here in the past 11,000 years, don't you think that, somewhere, they had places that were sacred to them?"

"I know they do," he said.

"Well . . .?"

"I guess it's as good an explanation as any," he said finally. "Though none of our native friends have come forward with any reports . . ."

Avery grinned. "That's what happened, I'm sure of it," she said. "The water ran across sacred ground and picked up some of the magic."

"But the animals in the display cases couldn't have been touched by the water," her dad said. "It merely lapped around the outside of the building."

"Doesn't matter," Avery said. "I've been thinking about this. The water touched the building and as soon as it did, the magic . . . moved into the animals."

Her mom smiled. "I think it covers all of the bases," she said.

Her dad shrugged. "As well as anything."

"And now they're all alive and . . ." She sucked in a breath. "Who's feeding them?! *What* are they feeding them? And there are carnivores with the herbivores! Are they attacking each other?"

"That's another odd thing," her dad said. "All of them seem to be getting along as though they had been raised together. Better than litter mates." He snorted. "It makes no sense. Those displays were really just carefully-preserved animal hides stretched over wooden or plastic forms or stuffed with straw and sewn shut! And given glass eyes!" He shook his head. "How could they be alive?!"

Chapter Two

Avery's dad tromped suddenly on the brakes and the car slid to a stop.

Avery rubbed her forehead where it had bumped onto the dashboard. "Gee, Dad . . ." she began. Then she realized that he was staring ahead at something. She turned to look out the front window. "Oh," she said.

A crowd of people had gathered, completely choking the street. Every head was craned as they all tried to see something somewhere ahead. Avery could see the flashes of cameras in the crowd.

Her dad pulled the car over to the curb and shut off the engine. "I don't like the look of this," he said. He opened his door and stepped to the pavement. "I guess we'll be all right to leave it here for a while," he said.

Avery followed him as he began to force his way through the strangely-quiet crowd. He glanced back at her as they slowly made their way. As they grew nearer to the museum, the crowd became heavier and nearly impossible to move through.

Suddenly, her dad broke through the last of the people and stopped, staring.

Avery pushed through to him. Then she, too stopped.

Every inch of the roof and most of the lawns around the museum were covered by birds and animals, all sitting or lying about, soaking up the warm early-morning sun.

"Michael!" Both of them turned as the museum custodian, Ben, followed by two park rangers, hurried over from where they had been standing near the great totem pole.

"Hi, Ben," her dad said, his voice faint. "Ummm . . . do you have any idea what happened?"

Ben turned to look at the museum. "Well, as nearly as I can guess," he said, "It looks like one of the larger animals smashed through the doors and the rest of them followed the leader out into the yard."

Avery's dad looked at the front doors, obviously the worse for the wear. Both had lost their glass and one was hanging by a single hinge. He took a deep breath and let it out. "But why are they still here?" he asked. "Why haven't they . . . escaped?"

Ben shook his head. "I really couldn't say," he said. "It makes no sense. But then, this whole situation makes no sense."

"True," Avery's dad said. He looked at Avery. "Well, honey, you wanted a look," he said. "I guess this is the best look you'll ever get!"

Ben smiled down at her. "Hi, Avery," he said. "Is it Bring-Your-Daughter-to-Work-Day?"

Avery laughed. "When your dad's museum work suddenly comes to life, it is," she said. She moved a couple of steps closer.

"Careful, miss!" one of the rangers warned. He smiled at her, then turned back toward the animals. "Wild animals are . . . how can I put this . . . wild!"

Just then, four RCMP officers broke through the crush of people and hurried toward them.

"What's going on here?" one of them asked. He turned to the rangers. "Do you men need some assistance?"

The ranger shrugged. "Your guess is as good as mine, Constable Talmadge," he said. "These animals aren't what they appear to be."

Talmadge frowned and looked around. "What do you mean? They look pretty normal to me."

Just then a large trout 'swam' placidly past them in the air. Talmadge's mouth fell open. "Is that . . .?" he managed finally.

"Umm . . . I guess it is," Avery's dad said.

The entire crowd went silent as all eyes stared.

Suddenly something else moved. A huge bear stood up and stretched. The birds that had been sitting on it flapped and tried to keep their balance.

All of the officers instantly forgot the fish and scrambled for their guns. They tried to herd Avery and her group back into the crowd.

"You people!" one of them said loudly. "You need to . . ."

Avery's dad touched him on the shoulder. "Maybe I should explain," he said. He briefly filled them in.

"Are you trying to tell me that these animals are the same ones who *were* the displays? In there?" Talmadge nodded toward the museum.

"I am," Avery's dad said.

"That's insane!" one of his companions said.

"But true," Ben said, stepping up beside Avery's dad. The officers stared at the two men.

At that moment, Ms. Kennard pushed her way through the crowd. "Man, what a crush!" she said, straightening her jacket and brushing at an imaginary bit of lint. "What is the . . .?" she glanced around and stopped. "Michael, did you . . . why did you let all of the animals out?"

"I didn't!" Avery's dad said. "I found them like this when I arrived!"

"Great!" Ms. Kennard said, looking disgusted.

"You know about this?" Talmadge asked her.

She sighed. "I do, officer," she said. "I had just hoped to keep it under wraps until we figured out what to do!"

He shook his head and looked around at all of them. "So, in your opinion, do these animals pose any sort of a threat to the people here?"

"Well, I don't know if . . ." Avery's dad began.

"No, sir," Ben said. "I've been watching them. They aren't aggressive to each other at all and certainly haven't shown any interest in the people." He waved an arm. "In fact, they don't seem to eat at all. No one is grazing and the carnivores who would normally be feasting on the smaller animals simply aren't interested." He smiled. "And, believe me, if I hadn't had a meal in over a century, *that* would be the first thing I would be thinking of!"

Talmadge turned to the others and they had a quick, whispered conference. Finally he shrugged.

"Well, we'll advise the people to move on," he said. "And we'll remain here, just in case." He nodded to the others and they moved toward the crowd. "I'm going to assume that these animals are under your supervision?"

"Actually . . . umm . . . okay," Avery's dad said, unwillingly.

Avery looked up at him. "The animals haven't reacted at all to the people. Why are you worried?"

But as she spoke, the large bull elk standing just outside the front doors suddenly lifted his head and turned in her direction.

All of them froze as the great deer began to move slowly toward them. As he grew closer, Avery's dad and the officers tried to push her behind them, but she resisted.

A few paces short of them, the huge animal came to a halt, his eyes on Avery.

Suddenly, Avery stiffened.

"What is it?" her dad said.

"Did you hear that?" she whispered.

Her dad frowned and peered about. "Hear what?"

Avery blinked. "That!"

Her dad shook his head. "I don't hear anything," he said.

"It's . . . not words exactly. More like . . . pictures in my head," Avery said.

"You can 'hear' pictures?" her dad asked.

"Yes . . . no . . . it's rather strange."

Avery looked up at the elk standing in front of her as it slowly dipped its head. She gasped. "I know what he's thinking!" she said.

Her dad looked at her. "What are you talking about?" he asked.

"The elk! I know what he's thinking!"

"How can you . . .?"

"Shh, Dad, just a moment . . ." Avery stared at the huge animal. Then she nodded and smiled.

"What is it thinking?" her dad whispered loudly.

"He thought all of the animals in his charge would like a bit of sun," Avery said. "That's why he opened the door for them."

"Oh, so the big guy's the one who broke my doors!" her dad said. The elk turned and looked at him.

"I think he's sorry about the doors," Avery said. "He's not used to turning knobs and no one was there to help."

"Are you trying to tell me that if any of us had been around, 'he' would have asked politely and waited while someone opened the door for him?"

Avery smiled as the great bull nodded. "Umm . . . yes," she said.

"He told you that?!"

"Yes," she said again.

"Now I've heard – and seen – everything!" her dad said. "Animals who have been dead for over a century suddenly come to life. Bears and wolves and deer and who-knows-what-all move in together peacefully. And now they can talk to humans?!"

The elk looked at him again, then turned back toward Avery.

"He says they have been friends a long time," she said. "But this is the first time they've been . . . together physically."

"Right. Of course I'm just guessing here, but it was probably because they were *dead*!" Her dad was beginning to look lost.

Avery turned to the elk for a moment. Then she turned back to her dad. "Only their bodies were dead," she said.

"What's that supposed to mean?" her father demanded.

"Well, he means that their spirits were never far away," Avery said. "At least I think that's what he said."

Her dad snorted. "Well, it all sounds like hooey to me!" he said.

Ben broke in. "I'm afraid that what we think – or thought – really doesn't matter anymore," he said. "I mean . . . look!"

All of them gazed across the dozens of animals and birds resting on the building and lawns.

Avery's dad shrugged. "You do have a point," he said, finally.

Suddenly, Avery nodded. "Okay," she said.

"What?" her dad asked. "What's going on?"

"They're going to go back inside now," Avery said. "Hehaka thinks they've had enough sun for today."

"I'd say so," her dad said. "The last thing you want to expose a mounted animal to is the sunlight. It dries out the hides and the stitches."

"Yeah, I don't think those worries apply any more," Ben said.

Suddenly, Avery's dad stopped and looked at her. "Hehaka?" he said.

"I think it means 'elk'," Avery said. "It's what he calls himself."

"Ah!" her dad said as he started walking again. "Of course."

Chapter Three

Avery followed Hehaka toward the building with her father and Ben trailing close behind. The RCMP officers remained where they were, disbursing the crowd and obviously nervous and trying to decide if they should be doing something more.

Avery and her new friend stood back while the other animals, birds and insects made their way inside. Then they followed, with Avery's dad and Ben right behind them.

As the humans came in from the bright sunlight, they paused for a moment to let their eyes adjust to comparative gloom.

Suddenly, a large, furry animal rose up beside Avery. A bear!

Unconsciously, she squeaked in alarm and jumped, colliding with Hehaka.

Before either of the men could react behind her, the bear dropped to all four feet and stared into Avery's eyes. Then sauntered away, making strange coughing noises in its throat.

"Oh, man, I thought we were done for!" Avery's dad said, reaching her side and throwing a protective arm belatedly around her. Then, "What are you . . . are you laughing?"

Avery turned to look at her father, blue eyes dancing. "Do you know what he said?" she asked.

"I really don't," he said.

"He said *Boo!*" she looked after the large animal. "And now, I think he's laughing."

Her dad just scratched his head. "Curiouser and curiouser, said Alice," he said.

Avery looked around. "Wow, this place is a mess," she said.

Hehaka looked at her.

"Yes, we'll get right on that," she said.

"Get right on what?" her dad asked.

"Hehaka wants us to clean this place up," Avery said.

"Oh, he does, does he?" her dad said. "Well, considering he and his friends were the ones who messed it up, maybe they could help us?"

Hehaka looked at him, then at Avery.

She smiled. "He says he's sorry about that," she said. "It was the only way to get his friends out before the water started coming in."

"Yeah, well, it really didn't," her dad said. "Come in, I mean."

"But they had no way of knowing if it would," Avery said.

Her dad sighed. "Right," he said. He walked toward the custodial closet. "I guess we might as well get busy," he said.

For the next few hours, Avery, her dad and Ben swept up glass and vacuumed floors. Finally, they stood back and surveyed their work.

The linoleum floors had been scrubbed clean and looked much, much better.

"Now for the upper floor!" Avery said.

"I can only guess at the mess up there!" her dad said.

Ben nodded.

Avery started for the staircase.

Her dad put out a hand and stopped her. "Not so fast, missy!" he said. "We need to make our presence known."

"Dad," Avery said. "Don't you think they already know we're here?"

All of them looked at the animals peering down at them from the upper story.

Her dad shrugged. "I guess you're right," he said.

Avery looked at Hehaka.

The great elk nodded and, suddenly, the animals began to pour out of the second floor, past the humans and into the reading room and activity rooms beyond. Soon the staircase and upper floor were deserted.

"Ready?" Avery said, lifting the vacuum. She quickly climbed up the staircase, noticing as she went that the animals had made surprising little mess during their occupation of the upper floor. There was some dust and hair, but nothing 'icky'.

Her father shook his head. "Stranger and stranger," he said. He turned to flip on a light, then jumped.

The great buffalo head on the wall had turned to look at him.

"Oh, man it scared me!" he gasped, putting one hand on his heart.

Avery walked over. Then she smiled and nodded.

"Is *he* talking to you now?" her dad asked.

She nodded again. "He's a little confused about why he can't move," she said.

Her dad frowned. "I guess I would be too," he said finally. "If I woke up and found myself with no body and stapled to a wall!"

Avery laughed and reached out to rub the great, furry head. "Huh!" she said. "He's warm!"

Her dad joined her. He glanced at the 'Do Not Touch' sign and snorted. Then he placed his hand alongside hers. "Feels nice, doesn't he?" he asked.

"He does!" Avery said. She stared into the eyes of the animal for a moment. Then nodded and reached around to scratch behind his left ear.

"Oh, come on! You're not going to tell me that he told you where to scratch!"

"Actually, he did!" Avery said, grinning.

The great bull stretched out his neck as far as he could, eyes half-closed in pleasure.

Avery's dad looked around and realized that all of the animal heads on the walls were blinking. Moving.

"This is so bizarre!" he said. Suddenly, he grinned. "You've probably heard people say 'Now I've seen everything', but you know they really haven't?" he asked. "Seen everything, I mean."

Avery stared at him. "Yeah?"

"Well, we have!"

Chapter Four

Avery's dad dropped the newspaper to the table and reached for his fork. "Well, I guess word is well and truly out," he said.

Avery glanced down at the large front-page picture in the Calgary Herald. It was an excellent, four-colour shot of the Banff Park Museum animals as they happily basked in the sunshine outside their home.

"So have they decided what to do?" Avery's mom asked.

Her dad shook his head as he passed the plate of crusty garlic bread to her mom. "They are still scratching their heads. Some of the board members are recommending that they all go to zoos. But there's no way these animals can go to a conventional zoo. They are anything but conventional."

"I think they need to be kept here!" Avery said, spearing a green bean viciously. "I mean, think about it! Visitors come from all over the world to see these animals! And none of the animals need to be fed or cleaned – or even caged?!"

Her dad chewed thoughtfully and swallowed. "Mmm . . . good lasagna, hon!" he said.

"Dad!" Avery said.

He looked at her. "You make some very good points, honey," he said. "But there would be a few things to consider before such a thing could happen. Not the least of which is . . . where?"

"Couldn't they just stay where they are?"

"They are much too crowded where they are," her dad said. He reached for a second slice of bread.

"Hmm . . ." Avery took a bite of lasagna. "Isn't there somewhere else . . .?

"Avery! Please swallow before you speak!" Avery's mom looked annoyed.

"Sorry, Mom!" Avery mumbled. She chewed and swallowed. Then showed her mother her empty mouth.

Her mom rolled her eyes.

"Isn't there somewhere else they could be put?" Avery asked.

"Not that I can think of," her dad said. "There's very little building allowed on park land and everything existing is in use or spoken for."

Avery frowned and stuffed the last of her garlic bread into her mouth.

"I think Avery is right, Michael," her mom said, shoving her empty plate aside and propping her elbows on the table. "Think about it! These are animals that people worldwide are hoping merely to catch a glimpse of. You've seen the traffic jams when a mother deer and her babies venture into view. And the crowds of people photographing birds and squirrels and even the common gophers. And the sheer number of visitors who get themselves into serious trouble every year because they have been raised on Disney animals and have the mistaken notion that the bear or cougar they see isn't going to have them for lunch."

"What are you saying?" Avery's dad said.

"I'm saying that this would give them the chance to get up close and personal with these animals without risking life and limb," her mom said.

Avery's dad frowned thoughtfully.

"Imagine the thrill of being able to pet one of the great grizzlies!" Avery said. "Or even a big-horn sheep! And to never, never have to worry that they will take a swipe at someone."

"How can you be so sure . . .?" her dad began.

"Dad, I've been talking to them all day," Avery said. "I know what they're thinking!"

Her mother looked at her. "That is the most fascinating part of all of this!" she said. "Tell me. What is it like?"

Avery frowned. "It's not really words," she said. "More like pictures."

"Pictures?"

"Yeah. They show me pictures."

"Can you think of an example?"

"Weeelll . . ." Avery rubbed her nose. "When I was talking to the eagle, he showed me the picture of an eagle with its wings held up into the air."

"Flying?" her mother asked.

"No. Just sitting there with his wings in the air," Avery said. "Then he showed me the eagle lowering its wings and moving them about as if they had gotten stiff and sore."

"But what did it mean?" her mom asked.

"Well, I figure he had been sitting there for I don't know how many years with his wings up in the air and he was very relieved and happy when he was able to move them."

"Oh." Her mother frowned. "Makes perfect sense."

Avery then told her mother about the trick the bear had played.

"Really?" her mom whispered, shocked. "I'd have had a heart attack!"

"Yeah. Like her father nearly did!" Avery's dad said. "That bear has quite a sense of humour!"

Avery was quiet for a moment. "The thing is," she said at last, "I know what these animals are thinking. They aren't mean or scared or hungry. They just want to be . . . friends."

Her dad looked at her. "Would you trust them, honey?" he asked.

"I would. Completely!"

Her mom smiled. "I guess that's your answer, then," she said.

[25]

Chapter Five

"Do you think I will be able to hear them?" Avery's
friend Hanna asked, bouncing excitedly on the car seat.

Avery smiled as Hanna's short, curly red hair
bounced with her. "I don't know," she said. "No one else
has been able to so far."

"I hope I can!" Hanna said, crossing her fingers and
screwing her face up tight.

"Well, we'll soon see," Avery's dad said from the
driver's seat. "Here we are!"

Avery and Hanna craned their necks to see over the
front seat. "Oh, they're outside again!" Avery said.

The animals and birds were once more taking
advantage of the warm summer sun. The sidewalk was
thronged with people, many of whom were moving out
among the animals, patting one, then another.

"What a place for an animal lover," Avery's dad said.

"Like us!" Avery said.

Her Dad pulled over and stopped the car. "There are
several people from the Wildlife Foundation here today,"
he said. "They are here to study the animals. Try not to get
in their way!"

"We won't," Avery said. "C'mon, Han, let's go see!"
The two girls jumped from the car and sprinted toward the
animals.

"Go slow!" Avery's dad shouted. "You really don't
know . . ."

Avery tossed a "We'll be careful, Dad!" over her
shoulder. Then, "Look! There's Mato!" she shouted as one
of the large bears turned and looked at them. "He's the one
I told you about. The one that's so funny."

"I'd like to meet him," Hanna said.

"You will," Avery said. "But first I need to introduce
you to Hehaka." She stopped and looked around. "I don't
see him, though."

The two girls made their way carefully through the sunning animals and birds, finally arriving at the door.

Avery peered inside. "Huh. I don't see him here, either," she said. She straightened and looked around.

Just then, the tall elk appeared from around the side of the Museum. It spotted Avery and turned toward them.

"Ah, Hehaka," Avery said, grabbing Hanna's hand and towing her over to the huge animal. "Hehaka," she said, "This is my best friend, Hanna!"

The big elk looked at Hanna, then at Avery.

Avery smiled. "He likes your hair," she said.

Hehaka tipped his head and turned back to Hanna once more. Then he looked at Avery again.

Avery nodded. "Best friends, yeah," she said.

"What did he say?" Hanna asked, bumping Avery's shoulder excitedly with the heel of her hand. "What did he say? Does he like me?!"

Avery looked at Hehaka, who dipped his head again. She smiled. "He does!" she said.

Hehaka turned to Hanna and stared into her eyes. Suddenly, her head came up. "I heard that!" she said. She glanced at Avery, then back to the tall elk. "I heard what he said!"

"Well . . . what did he say?" Avery asked, grinning.

"He said that friends are very important!" Hanna said. "I heard him!"

Both girls started jumping up and down and squealing excitedly. "Come on! Let's see if you can talk to Mato!" Avery said. She grabbed her friend's hand and pulled her back through the animals to the great grizzly, lying on his back in the sun not far from the front doors.

Avery felt her friend's hesitation as they grew closer to the great, furry animal. "Don't worry," she said. "He wouldn't hurt us!"

They stopped beside him and waited.

But the bear showed no sign that he was aware of their presence. He sighed and snorted in his sleep.

"Mato!" Avery said, softly.

No response.

"Mato!" she said a bit louder.

"Haven't you ever heard stories about people waking sleeping bears?" someone asked.

Avery looked up.

Her father was standing on the other side of the bear, briefcase in hand, looking disgusted.

"Yeah, but those were stories about 'normal' bears," she said. "And Mato is anything but normal!"

Her dad shrugged. "You've got me there," he said. "But I still think you should be careful!" He frowned, then shrugged and went into the museum.

Avery stepped closer and touched the bear on the nose.

Then she realized that the great bear's eyes were partially open. As she looked, one closed in a wink.

"Mato, you *are* awake," Avery said. "Quit kidding!"

The bear opened both eyes and looked at the two girls. Then he rolled onto his great paws and stretched and yawned, showing every one of his wickedly sharp teeth. Finally, he looked questioningly at Hanna.

"Mato, this is my best friend, Hanna," Avery said.

Mato grunted and Hanna gasped. "Not really!" she said, beginning to back away.

"What?" Avery asked.

"He just told me that I'd make a lovely dessert after he finished with my friend, the main course!"

Avery laughed. "I'll go get the ketchup," she told the bear.

Mato made some strange, grunting noises in his throat.

"He's laughing!" Hanna said.

"He does that a lot," Avery told her, smiling.

Mato and sat back onto his haunches. Then he looked at Hanna once more.

"In a house over there," Hanna answered, pointing. "Not too far from Avery's place."

The bear followed her pointing finger, then nodded.

"He says it must be nice to have somewhere to go," Hanna said.

Avery looked at the museum, then around at the animals who called it home. The sheer number was staggering. "Hmm. It must be quite crowded for them," she said.

Mato looked at her and nodded.

"Gee, do you think your dad will let him come home with me?" Hanna asked excitedly.

"Probably not," Avery said. "He wouldn't let him come with me."

"Oh." Hanna frowned. "Rats."

Just then the trout 'swam' past.

"Umm . . . Is that a fish?" Hanna asked.

"That trout is the weirdest thing about all of this," Avery said. "At least the other animals and birds and insects are in their natural habitat. Ground. Air. This crazy fish isn't even swimming in water!"

"H-how do you explain that one?" Hanna's voice trembled slightly.

"We really haven't explained any of this yet," Avery said. "I have my ideas, but nothing really covers that fish."

"Maybe it's just part of the magic," Hanna said.

"I think you're exactly right," Avery said. "But how? Or why?" She shrugged. "We don't know."

Hanna followed the fish for a few steps, then reached out and touched it. The fish turned and swam a circle around her. She let her fingers trail over it as it slid past. "Huh. It's smooth and cool," she said. "Like a fish."

Avery snorted. "Well, I do hope it's not warm and furry!" she said. She grinned. "That would just be weird!"

The two girls looked at each other and laughed.

For the next hour, they wandered through the lounging animals and birds, careful not to step on anything or anyone who might unwittingly wander into their path.

A tiny hummingbird appeared in front of them.

"Why, hello, little fellow!" Avery said, reaching out a hand. The bird hovered for a moment, then perched on her finger.

She looked down and it, then stroked its breast feathers with a gentle finger. Then she frowned. "Slower, my friend," she said. "I can't understand."

The bird ruffled its feathers.

Avery shook her head. "Slower."

It stilled.

"Just a bit slower. I think I've almost got it."

The bird stood still for only an instant, then tiny wings began to beat once more. It lifted off its perch and sailed up into the air.

"What did it say?" Hanna asked.

"I think he just told me his name," Avery said. "Wanbli Cikala."

"Any idea what that means?"

Avery smiled. "Little eagle!" she said.

Hanna laughed.

"Hey, Avery! Hanna!"

The girls looked up. Three of their friends, dark-haired and slender Phil, short and fiery Jessie and heavy-set, blonde Stuart were standing on the sidewalk next to the street.

"Hi, guys!" Avery said, waving. "Come on over!"

The two boys each linked arms with Jessie and pulled her from the crowded sidewalk onto the walkway in front of the museum. Then the three of them made their way over to Avery and Hanna.

"Wow! This is amazing!" Phil said. "I've lived here all my life and I've never seen anything like this!

"It's almost . . . magical!" Jessie said.

Stuart looked at her. "Magical?" he said.

"What is it with boys and magic?" Avery asked. "C'mon, guys, you both read Harry Potter!"

"I hate to tell you this, Ave, but Harry Potter isn't real!" Stuart said.

"Okay, you explain it," Avery said, indicating the animals around them.

Stuart looked around. "Hmmm . . ."

"Exactly!" Avery said.

"Wait, I haven't come up with anything yet!"

"Well tell us when you do!" Hanna said. "C'mon, Ave, let's go meet some more animals!"

"Wait for me!" Jessie said, following behind. "*I* believe in magic!"

"And me!" Phil said as he and Stuart started after them.

The five friends stopped as the great grizzly suddenly appeared in front of them.

"Oh, Geeze!" Stuart said, jumping back.

"It's okay!" Avery said, reaching out and scratching the huge animal under his chin. "He's a friend!"

"You're a big teddy bear, aren't you, Mato?" Hanna said as she, too started scratching.

The bear looked at the other kids.

"He's wondering why you aren't scratching him," Avery said, grinning.

"Wha – I think there's more than enough now," Phil said uncertainly.

"Come on! He won't bite!"

Suddenly both boys started to laugh.

"What?" Avery said. "What is it?"

"He said '*much*'!" Stuart doubled over with laughter.

"What?" Avery looked from the one to the other.

"You said 'he won't bite' and he said 'much'," Phil said, wiping a tear from his eye.

Avery shook her head. "That sounds like him!"

"You can hear him?" Jessie said.

"Can't you?" Stuart said. He turned to the huge animal. "Bear . . ."

"His name is Mato," Hanna said.

Stuart started again. "Mato," he said. "Say something to Jessie, please."

The bear swung his head back and forth, confused.

"Oh, I'm sorry," Avery said. "I should have introduced them." She pointed to Jessie. "This is our friend, Jessie," she said. "And this is Phil. And Stuart."

"Should we bow?" Phil asked. "Offer to shake hands?" He looked down at the bear's huge paws and sharp claws. "Maybe not."

Avery and Hanna laughed.

"Just talk to him," Avery said. "He's looking for friends."

"Well, I'd rather be his friend than his lunch!" Stuart said.

The bear looked at him.

"Hey!" Stuart said. "I'm not *that* big!"

"What did he say?" Jessie asked.

"Mato just told Stuart he'd be enough for lunch *and* dinner," Avery said.

All of them laughed.

"Mato, say something to Jessie," Avery said.

The great grizzly stood up on his hind legs and walked over to the small girl.

"Avery?!" Jessie said uncertainly, backing away.

"Don't worry," Avery said. "Just remember that he has a great sense of humour!"

"I . . . I'm trying to . . ." Suddenly, Jessie stopped and stared at the bear. "Really?" she said.

"What did he say?"

"He said I'm a very nice-looking creature. For a human."

All of them laughed again.

Mato dropped back onto his paws and started toward the open museum doorway. The other birds and animals got to their feet.

"Uh-oh, looks as though everyone is heading for home," Avery said.

Just as the grizzly reached the door, someone appeared from the other side.

The person squeaked briefly in alarm and backed out of sight. Then the five friends heard Ms. Kennard say, "Oh, I don't know if I'll ever get used to that!" The woman reappeared in the doorway, walking gingerly around the bulk of the great bear. Several other people followed her.

Mato calmly disappeared inside.

"Well, let's see if we can get things going," Ms. Kennard said, shaking hands with each of the others.

The group marched up the sidewalk and disappeared in the constantly-moving flow of pedestrian traffic.

Avery's dad appeared in the doorway. "Avery! Could you and . . ." he paused, realizing that her other friends had joined Avery and Hanna. ". . . your friends please come in here? I'm in the library."

"Sure, Dad!" Avery said.

The five friends skirted a flock of birds that were fluffing their feathers on the warm concrete just outside the door. One bird startled them by exploding into flight as they approached.

Avery watched it as it flew into a nearby tree. "Huh. I wonder what happened to that one?" she asked.

"Maybe it's a normal bird," Phil suggested. "And it thought it was joining a normal flock."

"Of course!" Avery said. "And it still thinks it has to escape when people get too close. Poor thing!" She stood back to let the others go ahead. Then they walked through the library entrance to the right and over to Avery's dad, who was sitting at one of the tables, reading something.

"What did you want, Dad?" Avery asked.

He looked up and set the piece of paper down. "Oh, Avery," he said. "I thought you would be interested in what has been proposed," he said. He glanced around at the birds and animals now entering through the front doors.

"What?" Avery asked.

"The members of the board have been discussing the possibility of closing one of the new ice arenas over at the center," he said. "And using the space as a sort of 'petting zoo' for our animals."

"Dad! That would be wonderful!" Avery said. "Then they could stay right here!"

"Well, the idea depends on a few things."

"Yeah?" Avery said.

"Well, first of all we'd have to get it past the town fathers," he said.

"Okay. And the next thing?"

"Well, we'd have to get it past the people who use the arena." He smiled. "Of those two, I think *that* one will be the most difficult."

"Yeah, I play hockey and there is already a shortage of ice time – with two arenas and the outdoor one in the winter!" Phil said. "Our team had to practice as 6:00 A.M. most days."

"Well, it's good for you," Avery's dad said. "Teaches you to start your day early!"

"Ugh!" Phil said.

"But think of being able to visit the animals!" Avery said. "To be right there with them! It will be unlike any zoo in the world!"

"You don't have to convince me, honey, my thinking is the same," her dad said. "People come from all over the world in hopes of catching even a glimpse. Particularly of the bears. And we would have them here, not only to see, but to actually interact safely with."

"I know which choice I'd make," Stuart said. "If it was between sports or animals."

"Yeah, well everyone knows you don't like sports, Stuart!" Jessie said. "So I'm afraid that doesn't mean much!"

Stuart shrugged.

"Another hitch in my plan is that our 'arena' solution could only be temporary," Avery's dad said. "Sooner or later, preferably sooner, we'd have to build the animals a real facility. Something specifically suited to their needs."

"Oh," Avery said. "So . . . expensive."

"Incredibly expensive," her dad said.

"Where would we get that kind of money?" Phil asked.

"Well, there could be some government money," Avery's dad said, rather doubtfully.

Avery looked at her dad's face. "But that wouldn't get the whole thing built, would it?" she asked.

He shook his head. "Probably only get us halfway to our goals."

"So what else could we do?" Avery asked.

"Well, there are always big companies who are eager to get their names up on important buildings," her dad suggested. "And I think we could approach some of them."

"Could *we* do some fund-raising?" Phil asked.

Avery's dad nodded. "That was my next suggestion," he said. "There are many ways to fund-raise. Maybe your school would like to get involved." He smiled. "After all, the Banff Park 'Zoo' will probably become a substitute classroom."

"That's the best thought of all!" Stuart said, enthusiastically.

"So how do we get this started?" Avery asked.

"I'll draw up a plan," her dad said. He pursed his lips. Then, "And there was one other thing I wanted to talk to you about," he said. He scratched his neck and looked at

Avery. "This is just from me, but if we should get this project off the ground, would you and Hanna be able to help out? Sort of be the unofficial gamekeepers?"

"WHAT?!" Avery shouted.

Her dad covered one ear. "Ah! Avery!"

"Sorry dad," Avery said, a little more subdued. "What?"

"Well, I figured because you and Hanna can, you know, talk to . . ."

"And Phil, Stuart and Jessie," Avery put in.

It was her dad's turn. "What?"

"Yeah. *All* of us can talk to them," Avery said.

"Even me!" Jessie said.

Avery's dad looked around at the five eager faces. "Really? You can *all* talk to them? Well, that's great!" He frowned. "All kids," he said, mostly to himself. "I wonder why it doesn't work with the adults?"

"Maybe it's just a 'kid' sort of thing," Avery said.

"Hmmm." Her dad shrugged. "Well, that makes my job even easier," he said. "I'm going to go to the board and discuss having you – all – act as unofficial gamekeepers for the animals. Make sure they're safe and happy."

"I'm sure we can do that!" Avery said. "What do you guys think?"

Avery's dad clapped both hands over his ears as the walls shook with their enthusiastic response.

Chapter Six

"Do you think they'll give us uniforms?" Stuart asked
excitedly. The five friends had plopped down on two of the
benches in front of the museum.

Only a few of the animals remained outside. The rest
had disappeared back inside their home.

"I think we're a long way from uniforms," Avery
said. "We aren't even sure this is going to happen, yet!"

"But do you think . . .?"

"Stuart!" Jessie said. "I'm sure that if everything goes
through, they will give us uniforms. Or at least shirts or
something."

"I want my name on mine," Stuart said. "And our
group name . . . Guys!" he said. "We don't have a group
name, yet!"

"How about the Baby-Sitters Club?" Phil asked,
grinning.

"Umm, I think that's already taken," Jessie said. "I
used to read the books."

"I didn't really mean it!" Phil said. "Sheesh!"

"Stuart's right, though," Avery said. "We need a
name for our club. If it ever *becomes* a club."

"How about the *Animal Rescue Society* or *ARS* for
short?" Hanna said.

Avery wrinkled her nose. "Hmm . . . I guess it'd be
all right . . ."

"Except that we really aren't *rescuing* anyone," Phil
pointed out.

"How about the Friendly Animal Rangers Team?"
Stuart asked.

"Ha, right. And what would you have embroidered on
your sleeve?" Avery asked.

"F-A-R . . . oh," Stuart said. "Maybe not such a good
idea."

"How about the *Banff Animal Rangers*?" Phil asked. "*BAR*."

"Oh, you know, I like that one," Hanna said.

"Banff Animal Rangers . . . I like it too," Avery said. "And let's add *Club*. Because it's our club."

"Okay, everyone, we're the *Banff Animal Rangers Club*," Stuart said.

"Or *BARC* for short," Avery said.

"Perfect!" Hanna and Jamie said together.

"I guess we're all in favour!" Phil said.

Avery sighed. "Now, all that's left is to *become* a club," she said.

* * *

"We're meeting with a lot of opposition from the parents *and* from the government," Avery's dad said morosely, poking a fork into his salad. "The parents don't want to give up the arena they just got, even for a short while, and the government is on a retrenchment/austerity kick right now." He sighed. "Almost every person I talked to today agreed totally that such a facility was needed. Both to preserve the animals and to promote tourism."

"But?" Avery's mom asked.

"But actually building such a facility would take millions. And no one wants to try to get *that* past the voting public."

"Did you explain about the animals?" Avery asked.

"I don't think there's a person in this world who hasn't heard about our animals," her dad said tiredly. "And everyone agrees that they are of vital importance. They're even being referred to as Canadian *icons*. But so far, no one with any financial clout has come forward."

"That's so short-sighted," her mom said, passing the plate of chicken to Avery. "Just one piece, dear, I want to save the rest for some soup!" She looked back at Avery's dad. "Can't they see how good it would be for the tourist industry here?"

"Ummph!" Her dad took a swig of milk. "As one group is so happy to point out, the mountains are also great Canadian icons," he said. "And, according to that group, we get plenty of traffic from the skiers alone."

"Yeah. In the winter," Avery pointed out.

"Well, let's face it, we still get a lot of visitors in the summer," he went on.

Avery frowned. "I guess you're right."

Her dad grinned at her. "Of course I'm right. I'm your father!"

Avery's mom laughed. "If *that* was a sure thing . . ." she said.

"Never mind," her dad said, giving his wife a mock-glare. "Anyway, we're having an uphill climb."

"Not hard to do when you live in the mountains!" her mom said, brown eyes twinkling.

"Ha-ha."

"Well, I suppose I could talk to a few of my friends and we can see what we can organize," her mom said.

Her dad sighed. "Every little bit helps. If we could just get our temporary solution through, at least that would be a start." He frowned thoughtfully. "It is early days yet. And we do have a couple of people on town council who are on our side; who think that a facility to house these, quote: *'unique animals'* would be a good thing."

"So what's the hold up there?"

"The usual. Money," he said. "The biggest problem is that the other members of the council think the animals would be much better situated in Calgary. No problem building them housing there. Or they could even have their own facility in the zoo."

"But that would be awful!" Avery said. "They need to stay here! Where the tourists can see them in their natural habitat!"

"I should point out that they wouldn't be *in* their natural habitat," her dad said. "Even in their own facility."

"Well, you know what I mean!" Avery said. "Close to it! Or at least closer than Calgary!"

"You don't have to convince me, hon," her dad said. "I agree with you. It's just the powers-that-be who don't."

"Well, can't you do anything?" Avery asked.

"I'm doing all I can," her dad said. "Talking to people with influence. With money. It's a complex issue!"

"I think it's a simple issue," Avery said. "Keep the animals here!"

Her dad smiled at her. "We'll do our best, hon," he said.

"Well, I wish my friends and I could talk to them," Avery said. "We'd help them see the big picture! We could talk to them about what it means to us to actually be able to talk to 'wild' animals. To be their friends. To learn about them." She grinned. "I'm pretty sure there would be nothing like it in the world!"

Her dad smiled. "I'm pretty sure you're right!" he said. He tipped his head to one side. "Wait, that might be the solution!" he said. "Ave, would you and your friends care to make a presentation to the council?"

Avery stared at him. "Really?" she asked. "You want us to talk to them?"

"Yes. I think it would be a spectacular idea!" her dad said. "You could tell them just what you've been telling me!"

"Do you think it will help?"

"Well, it certainly wouldn't hurt!"

Chapter Seven

"Nervous?" Avery's dad was straightening Phil's tie.

"A little," Phil said.

"I think we're all a bit scared, Dad," Avery said. She took a large bite of her ice-cream sandwich.

"Careful not to get that on you, hon," her dad said, smiling. "Going in there with ice cream and chocolate all down the front of you probably wouldn't make a very good impression!"

Avery wiped her face with a napkin. "Sorry, Dad," she said. "But when I'm nervous, I eat!"

Jessie looked at her. "When I'm nervous, I *can't* eat!" she said.

"You'll probably be happy about that one day," Avery's dad said, grinning at the slender girl. He looked around at the rest of the kids. "Everyone ready?"

"As ready as we'll ever be," Stuart said, giving his suit jacket a jerk.

"Well, let's get over to the meeting!" Avery's dad said.

* * *

"Oh, man look!" Phil said. "We're not even on the agenda!"

Avery grinned at him and pointed to the first item.

"Oh," he said.

"You *are* nervous!" Hanna said.

Phil sighed. "Just a little," he said.

Hanna smiled. "A little more than a little!" she said.

Phil brushed at some imaginary dust on his sleeve and said nothing.

The group became quiet as more people shuffled into the room and found places around them or up at the front in the council members' seats.

Finally, the mayor called the meeting to order.

After some initial business concerning the agenda, the mayor looked down at Avery's dad. "I understand that you represent a delegation, Michael," she said. "Is your group ready to make their presentation?"

Avery's dad stood up. "We are, Mayor Sorenson," he said. He looked at the kids. "You're on!"

Avery and her friends got to their feet and gathered together in a tight knot in the space between the council seats and the audience.

Mayor Sorenson smiled. "Don't be nervous, kids," she said. "We won't bite."

Avery smiled and shook back her long, blonde hair. "Madame Mayor," she said. "We," she indicated her friends, "my friends and I, have come to talk to you about building a facility for the animals from the Banff Park Museum."

The mayor and council members nodded.

"We've had a chance to get to know these animals," Phil took over. "Spend time with them. Even talk to them."

"You can talk to them?" one of the councilors said.

Phil grinned. "We can, sir," he said. "All of us can."

"Excuse me, but what's that like?"

"Sort of like . . . pictures," Jessie spoke up. "Like seeing pictures in your head." She grinned. "We were talking to one of the hummingbirds, who talks very fast, and he kept showing us a picture of himself as a mighty eagle. A tiny, mighty eagle."

"His name is Wanbli Cikala," Avery said. "Which means Little Eagle."

"But if they speak in pictures, how do you know their names?" another councilor asked.

"A very good question," Stuart said. "The names just seem to . . . come into our heads."

The council members looked thoughtful.

"Anyways, we've spent a lot of time with them, and they have been very . . . informative about themselves and their former lives," Stuart said. "We think they could be a valuable tool for kids like us."

"Actually, for all people," Avery broke in. "I mean, think about it. Here are animals who will never, ever hurt anyone. Who can actually talk to people. Who never need any care or cages or even food! And then think about how many tourists had problems with wild animals last year because they do crazy things just to see them and get pictures with them." She grinned. "I've always wanted a live bear for a pet, but even the tamed ones are never – quite – tame. Imagine being able to cuddle with a full-grown grizzly and know he'd never hurt you!"

"I've always wanted a bear for a pet!" one of the councilors said.

"Shh!" another said.

"Well, I have!"

Avery looked around at her friends. "All of us can talk to these animals," she said. "We know what they are thinking and feeling. We would be happy to act as care-givers or tour guides or whatever you need."

"We think it is important that we keep these animals here in Banff, where they lived," Phil said. "Important to the tourists who come here and also important to those of us who live here and can learn from them."

"I have just one question," one of the councilors said.

The mayor looked at her. "Yes, Councilor Taylor?"

"We are agreed that everything that has happened is rather . . . magical," Councilor Taylor said.

The group nodded.

"I know from my extensive work with wildlife that it can be anything but predictable." she went on. "So, how do we know that magic – and animals - will be any different? How do we know that in a few days, or a few months, the magic won't just . . . disappear, and that we'll be left with the same interesting, but inanimate, mounted animals we had before?"

Avery and her group blinked. "Umm . . ." Avery said. She hadn't even thought about the magic just . . . ending. The though made her heart sink into her shoes.

"You don't know, do you?" Councilor Taylor said. "We could get this facility built and then quite suddenly have the magic end and then where will we be?" She smiled. "I don't mean to try to derail anything here," she said. "But I do think we need to . . . consider other possibilities, especially when we are talking the kind of numbers we will be talking."

"Thank you, Councilor Taylor," Mayor Sorenson said.

Avery spoke up. "I think we need to just go ahead based on what we know now," she said at last. "If we were to try to make decisions based on 'what might happen', we wouldn't get very much done." She sighed. "Thank you for listening to us," she added.

"And thank you for your very persuasive arguments," Mayor Sorenson said. "We will deliberate and get back to you in the next day or two."

"Thank you," Avery's dad said. He nodded toward the door and all of them filed out.

They were a very quiet group.

"Do you think the magic could disappear, Dad?" Avery asked. "Just disappear?"

Her dad frowned thoughtfully. "I don't know, hon," he said finally. "But I really don't think so. That magic has been safely stored in the sacred places for who knows how long. If it remained there, it will remain here."

"Until another storm-of-the-century washes it away!" Stuart said sourly.

Phil laughed. "The reason they call it a 'storm-of-the-century' is because it only happens once a century!"

"But what's to say that *this* storm of 2013 happened at the end of *this* century and that next year, 2014 is the beginning of *another* century?" Stuart said. "You could have two storms back to back and still technically be right!"

Avery looked at him. "Why do we listen to you?" she asked.

"Because I'm usually right," Stuart said smugly.

"Pffff!"

"Then I guess we'll just have to make sure we keep the animals out of any flood waters," Jessie said practically.

"Right!" everyone agreed.

"So, other than that last bit, I thought our presentation was good!" Phil said.

"I think you did an excellent job," Avery's dad said. "You certainly said all that needed to be said." He sighed. "Now all we can do is wait."

"Well, I could eat something," Jessie said.

Stuart looked at her. "I thought you couldn't eat when you were nervous."

Jessie grinned. "I'm not nervous now."

"I think all of us deserve a milkshake," Avery's dad said. "Let's go to Cows. I'm buying!"

* * *

An hour later, Avery and her dad met her mom as they came in their front door.

"So?" her mom asked. "Your text said it went well, but I want to hear it all!"

Avery's dad put his arm around Avery's shoulders. "You would have been proud of your daughter, Maureen," he said.

"I already am," her mom said. She looked from the one to the other. "So . . .?

Chapter Eight

"What's he doing?" Avery stopped walking and stared across the lawn.

"Who?" Hanna asked. Then she, too, saw the tall man standing quietly in the midst of the animals, eyes closed and hands half-raised. "Oh."

It had been nearly 12 hours since Avery and Hanna had been among their new animal friends and they had decided to walk down to the museum simply to spend some time with them.

"Umm . . . I don't know," Hanna said. "But the animals don't seem to mind at all."

"No," Avery said. "Come on. Let's go see!"

The two girls crossed the grass as quickly as possible while trying to avoid stepping on anything – or anyone – important.

They stopped beside the stranger.

"Excuse me," Avery said. "Can we help you with anything?"

The man opened his eyes and turned his head slowly. He was older than they had first assumed. His face was seamed with age. His hair, pulled back and twisted into a long braid was snowy white. "Hello, my sisters," he said, quietly, his face creasing into a wide smile and his black eyes twinkling. "Have you come to visit with our brothers and sisters, too?"

For the first time, Avery noticed that Hehaka and Mato, along with several others, were gathered around, watching the man intently. Obviously she and Hanna had interrupted something.

The man bowed politely. "Allow me to introduce myself, my sisters," he said. "My name is Seeking Eagle."

Avery put out her hand. "Nice to meet you, Seeking Eagle," she said. "Where are you from?"

"I go where the Great Spirit leads," Seeking Eagle said, shaking her hand. "I live where the Great Spirit whispers."

"Oh," Avery said. "I'd hate to try to write down *that* address."

Seeking Eagle smiled.

"So you came to see the animals?" Avery asked.

"They called to me," Seeking Eagle said. "And I answered."

"Really?" Hanna asked. "Why did they do that?"

"They have strong spirits," Seeking Eagle said. "Which have long roamed free. We have travelled together for many, many years."

"Travelled together?" Avery was feeling lost. "How, exactly?"

Seeking Eagle looked up and lifted a hand toward the sky. "When our brothers died, their spirits were released to wander. Eventually, they found me and we became companions." He looked toward the mountains surrounding them. "But when the magic waters came, their spirits were called back. Even as they were leaving, they made me promise that I would follow." He smiled. "I have," he said, simply. "I just travel much, much more slowly."

"So you know how they all came back to life," Avery said.

"I do," Seeking Eagle said. He looked around at the animals pressing close against him, then reached out with a gentle hand to touch one, then another. "It was the magic water," he said. "It surrounded their dwelling place and called to them."

"I knew it!" Avery said. "I knew it had something to do with the water!"

"And now they have a work to do."

"They . . . what?" Avery said. "Work?"

"Yes," Seeking Eagle said. "Their Great Work."

"What Great Work could they possibly have to do?" Avery asked.

Seeking Eagle smiled at the girls. "Each of us has a Great Work," he said. "And it is up to us to find what it is." He looked around at the animals. "I don't know what their Work is," he added. "But *they* will. When it's time."

Avery tipped her head to one side and looked at him. "What is your Great Work, Seeking Eagle?" she asked.

He smiled again. "Mine is simple," he said. "Go where the Great Spirit sends."

"And what do you do when you get there?"

"Whatever the Great Spirit directs."

Avery thought about that for a moment. Then, "Do you think the Great Spirit could tell you how to save these animals?" she asked. "I mean, if we can't find the money, we won't be able to build them a home. If we can't build them a home, out they go. To Calgary."

Seeking Eagle was silent for a moment. "They will be taken from here?" he asked, finally.

"Yes. Unless we can get enough money to build a home for them."

"But . . ." he looked at the museum behind them.

"This museum was fine for displaying the animals," Avery said. "Or at least a few of them. But for the tourists to be able to really see them and be with them . . ."

"Ah. I do see," Seeking Eagle said. "This beautiful building is . . . what would you say . . . inadequate."

"Totally."

"Ah." He frowned thoughtfully for a moment, then looked at the girls once more. "I will think on this," he said. He looked around. "The spirits of these animals are powerful. They have travelled far and are anxious to get on with their Great Work." He frowned. "Perhaps there is a way and the Great Spirit will whisper it to me."

"Ummm . . . Thanks?!" Avery said.

"Was that a question?" Hanna asked.

[48]

"No that was a 'thanks'. Thanks," Avery said.

Seeking Eagle bowed his head slightly, then turned back to the animals.

The two girls made their way carefully to the door of the museum.

"That was strange," Hanna whispered as they stepped inside.

"I thought he was amazing!" Avery whispered back.

"Amazing? Or weird?"

Avery laughed. "Maybe a bit of both." She pulled open the door of the museum and stood back to let Hanna precede her. Avery's dad was standing in the little admissions kiosk. "Hello, ladies," he said cheerfully. "May I interest you in a tour?"

Avery laughed and leaned on the desk. "Maybe," she said. "What do we get?"

"I can offer you a first-class view of several empty displays," he said. "As well as an up-close and personal introduction to several mounted animal trophies." He shook his finger. "I have to warn you, though, they have been known to move unexpectedly and even communicate." He frowned. "Except for one," he added.

"Really?" Avery said. "Which one?"

"That moose, there," her dad said, pointing toward the animals mounted on the upper walls of the second floor, just under the lantern windows.

The girls followed the pointing finger.

Avery gasped. Her father was right! All of the other animals were moving. Blinking. Only that moose was still.

As still as a . . . stuffed moose.

"Strange," she murmured. "I wonder why . . ." Then she shrugged and looked around at all of the other animal heads fastened to the walls throughout the building - the only animals not taking advantage of the sunshine outside - and shook her head. "The poor things," she said. "I don't know why people would do that."

Her father looked at her, "It never bothered you before," he said.

"I know. I mean, they were dead and didn't know any better," Avery said. "But now . . . when they know . . ." she shrugged.

"Don't worry about it honey," her dad said. "They don't really seem to be upset."

"How could you tell?!" Avery demanded, suddenly feeling . . . angry. "Have you spoken to them?"

"Well . . . no," her dad said.

"Harrumph!" Avery said.

"Was that a harrumph?" Hanna asked.

"No!" Avery said.

"It was! It was a harrumph! I didn't know people really did that!"

"They don't!" Avery said, her cheeks turning slightly pink as she moved away. Frowning, she walked to the staircase and began to climb.

"Where are you going, honey?" her dad asked.

"Up," Avery said.

"Ummm . . . why?"

"I'm going to see my new friend," she said. She reached the top of the stairs and moved across to the enormous bull bison on the wall. "*Hello, Sir Donald,*" Avery reached out and scratched him behind the ear. Then she laughed. "*Okay.*" She reached around and scratched behind his other ear.

Hanna climbed the stairs and joined her. Turning the scratching of the shaggy beast over to her, Avery walked across the room and returned with a wooden chair. She placed it in front of the bison and stood on it, then put her forehead against Sir Donald's.

"*Are you sad, Sir Donald?*" Then she smiled. "*No. Sad.*" She grinned briefly at her friend. "He thought I said 'bad'!" She leaned against him again. "*I know you're a big, bad boy, but are you mad that you can't do anything anymore?"*

The bull closed his eyes and seemed to be thinking. Then his eyes opened again and his head turned slightly. For several seconds, he stared into Avery's eyes.

Finally, "*Oh.*" She sat down on the chair.

"What did he say?" Hanna asked. "I couldn't understand it."

"He asked how he could be sad when every friend he's ever had is here with him," Avery said. She looked at Hanna. "I guess I see his point."

"So, prison isn't really prison if you're there with your friends?" Hanna asked.

"Exactly!" Avery said. "But . . . ugh!"

* * *

"I can't believe it!" Avery's dad said. "I simply can't believe it!"

"But I though our presentation went well!" Avery said, feeling near to tears. "How could they turn it down?!"

"Your presentation was great!" her dad said. "I don't know what they are thinking!"

"Perhaps that they can't afford such a project right now?" Avery's mom said.

Her dad snorted. "When you have something like this fall into your lap, you don't just ignore it," he said. "Do you know we've had everyone from biologists to geneticists to veterinarians prowling around the museum and poking and prodding the animals? This is the biggest thing to happen in the animal world since the cloning of Dolly the Sheep!" He sighed. "But the fact remains that they won't touch the project until we have money in hand to pay for it." He looked at his wife. "They've already started making arrangements to send the animals to Calgary!"

[51]

Chapter Nine

It was raining. Except for some seagulls and a few pigeons, the grounds around the museum were noticeably and understandably empty of wildlife.

Well, almost empty, Avery corrected herself as the huge trout slowly 'swam' past, obviously enjoying the moisture.

Carefully skirting the great fish, she dashed across the walk to the front door and, pulling it open, hurried inside. Considering the museum was crowded with at least one of every type of bird, animal and insect ever to live in the Rocky Mountains, the place was strangely quiet.

Rustling and shuffling and the occasional stamped hoof were the only discernible sounds.

Avery's dad and the custodian, Ben, were standing in the doorway to the library. Her dad glanced at her. "He's been there for an hour!" he stage-whispered to her, turning to stare upward.

Avery looked up.

Seeking Eagle was standing on top of the main cabinet where Hehaka and his friends had stood so long and so silently. By his gestures and the expression on his face, his thoughts were anything but silent. Several animals had moved closer to him and were looking at him, either through the bars of the second floor railing or over it. He looked at them, one at a time, and nodded.

Suddenly, Avery heard Mato's 'voice'. "*Where would they take us?*"

Seeking Eagle turned toward the great bear. "*To the great city to the east.*"

Hehaka pushed to the front. "*Cannot go.*"

"*But you must . . . if they can't . . .*"

"*Cannot go!*" Hehaka repeated.

Seeking Eagle was silent for a moment. Finally, "*Can*not *go?*"

Hehaka simply looked at him.

Seeking Eagle nodded. "*I understand.*" He took a deep breath. "*I have been speaking with the Great Spirit. I may have a plan.*"

He climbed down from the high cabinet and smiled at Avery. "Good afternoon, my sister," he said.

"What were you talking about?" Avery demanded. "You and the animals. You said you may have a plan!"

"Yes," Seeking Eagle said. "The Great Spirit has whispered it to me."

"Well, let's go, then," Avery said, turning toward the door.

Seeking Eagle stayed where he was. "It will not be easy," he said. "It will test you and your friends to your limits."

"Okay!" Avery said. "Let's get started!"

Seeking Eagle nodded. "Call your friends."

*   *   *

"You want us to do what?!" Stuart jumped to his feet and stared at Seeking Eagle as though the man had lost his mind.

"I want you to climb a mountain with me," Seeking Eagle said.

"Oh, no, man. I don't *do* mountains," Stuart said, sitting down once more. "Not for anyone."

"Would you do it for the animals?" Seeking Eagle asked.

Stuart stared at the man suspiciously.

"Maybe you'd better tell us what you have in mind," Hanna said quietly.

Seeking Eagle smiled. "The Great Spirit has told me of a place, not too far from here, that has been . . . prepared for you. For the animals."

"Really?" Avery said. "Where?"

"It is to the north," Seeking Eagle said. "The Great Minihapa."

"I don't know that mountain," Avery said.

"Cascade," Stuart said. "Honestly, Avery, don't you listen in school?"

Avery made a face at him, "You know I do, Stuart!" she retorted. "I'm always the one beating you!"

Stuart made a face back. "In your dreams!" he said.

Avery turned back to Seeking Eagle. "I've hiked Cascade lots of times," she said. "With my parents."

"So have I," Phil said.

"And me!" Jessie and Hanna added, speaking together.

Seeking Eagle smiled. "This will be a slightly different hike to the one you took with your families," he said. "This hike will challenge you."

"Ugh!" Stuart said. "I only live in the mountains. I don't get up close and personal with them!"

Seeking Eagle laughed. "Then I think it is about time I introduced you," he said. "Maybe you will discover, as I have, that they call to you!" He sobered. "We will need you for this task," he added quietly

Stuart looked at him. "Seriously?"

"Seriously," Seeking Eagle said.

Stuart sighed. "So when do we start?" he asked.

"As soon as I get permission from your parents," Seeking Eagle said.

* * *

"A hike up Cascade?" Avery's mom grinned. "We've done it many times with Avery."

"So you will give your permission for her to come with us?" Seeking Eagle said.

"Who all is going?" her dad asked.

"All my friends," Avery said. "Hanna, Jessie, Phil and Stuart."

"Stuart?! How did you convince him to go?" Her mom shook her head. "I think I'd pay money to see that boy climb up a mountain!"

"So can I?" Avery asked.

"*May* I?" her dad corrected.

Avery sighed. "*May* I?"

Avery's mom looked at Seeking Eagle, then at her husband. She raised her eyebrows questioningly.

"You will be guiding them, Seeking Eagle?" Avery's dad asked.

"I will," Seeking Eagle said.

Avery's dad nodded. "Good."

"I guess it would be all right," her mom said. "As long as you stay together and stay on the paths!"

"Goody!" Avery said, hopping up. "I'll get my backpack!"

* * *

"So what do we need to bring?" Stuart asked.

"We'll need the usual," Phil said.

"Okay, imagine that this is the first time I've done this," Stuart said. "Because it is. Then let's go from there."

Phil laughed. "Okay. Water."

"Check."

"Snacks and energy foods."

Stuart threw in some granola bars and a couple of pieces of fruit. "Check."

"First aid kit."

Stuart frowned. "Why would we need a first aid kit? Are we planning on getting injured?"

"No, we're just trying to plan for any contingency," Avery said.

Stuart looked at her, surprised. "That's an awfully big word for you, Ave," he said.

"I stayed up all night, memorizing words to impress you with, Stuart," Avery said. Then she

[55]

grinned. "My dad uses it all the time." She stuck out her tongue. "And so do I!"

Stuart left the room, returning shortly with a small, white container. He tossed it into his backpack. "Hope mom doesn't miss this," he said. "Anything else?"

"Better throw in a jacket, change of clothes and extra socks," Phil said. "I know it's July down here, but it's pretty cold and windy at the top of the mountain."

"Got it," Stuart said. "Anything else?"

"Compass?"

"Okay, why would you think that a person who's never hiked a day in his life would possibly have a compass?"

"Because you like gadgets," Avery said, grinning.

Stuart shrugged. "Right," he said.

A few minutes later, the three of them left Stuart's room and joined the rest of the group in the front hall.

"All packed?" Seeking Eagle asked.

"Yep," Stuart said. "Ready for anything."

"I do hope so," the elderly man said. "Let's go!"

* * *

The sun was just topping the eastern ridge when Avery's dad pulled up to the almost deserted parking lot at Mount Norquay. "Now don't forget anything," he said as Avery and her friends slid out and grouped around Seeking Eagle. "Especially don't forget to hike safe!"

"There's something very grammatically wrong with that statement," Stuart said, grinning at Avery's dad.

"Only you or Avery would have picked up on that, Stuart," her dad said, shaking his head. "But you know what I mean!"

"We'll be careful, Dad!" Avery said.

"I hope so," her dad said. "Don't forget to call Phil's mom when you get back here, okay? See you soon!"

"Bye!" everyone shouted. Then they turned to follow Seeking Eagle down the service road to the trail head.

Avery looked up at the great chair lifts as they trailed along below them. "It always creeps me out to see them sitting there, still and silent," she said. "Like the end of the world or something."

"Did you know that the Big Chair was built back in 1948 and is the second oldest chair lift in North America?" Stuart said. "After some lift in Vermont."

"I did not know that," Seeking Eagle said.

"It's pretty amazing that it's still in use," Stuart said.

"Amazing to *you*, Stuart," Jessie said, making a face.

"Well, I'm interested in things," Stuart said.

"Do not lose that thirst," Seeking Eagle said. "It will serve you well."

Stuart stuck his tongue out at Jessie and moved closer to their elderly guide.

For some time, the trail went downhill, and the walking was nearly effortless.

"Gee, I didn't realize that hiking was so easy!" Stuart said.

Phil smiled. "Oh, this is just the start, Stu," he said. "Wait till we start upping." He pointed up the mountain. "The amphitheater is somewhere up there!"

Stuart followed the pointing finger and sighed.

Avery smiled as they walked on.

By the time the group had reached Forty Mile Creek, Stuart had already emptied two of his water bottles.

"Better go easy on the water, brother," Seeking Eagle said. "Sometimes drinking too much can be just as dangerous as drinking too little." He stopped beside a bridge. "Fill up your water bottles here," he said. "This will be our last chance."

The kids crouched down and let the cool, clear water pour into their bottles.

"Mmm . . . best water in the world!" Phil said as he took a long drink. He knelt down and refilled his bottle, then capped it tightly.

"Ready?" Seeking Eagle asked. "Let's start hiking!"

Just past the bridge, the trees thinned for a moment and the hikers were suddenly given a spectacular view.

"That's Mount Louis," Stuart said, pointing. "And behind it over there? Mount Edith."

"Now that would be a climb!" Phil said.

"Yeah. I'm glad we're on this mountain," Hanna said, hitching up her backpack.

"How do you know the mountains if you've never been up here, Stu?" Jessie asked.

"I read!" Stuart said.

"The armchair explorer," Jessie said.

"Hey!" Stuart said.

Everyone laughed.

As the trail started to climb, conversation ceased as everyone concentrated on their footing and their breathing.

"Okay, now I know why I never do this," Stuart panted after a few minutes.

"Oh, we're just getting started!" Phil said.

"Thanks, Phil, that really helps," Stuart said, frowning at his friend.

Phil laughed.

"Now I want you to pay attention to your footing here," Seeking Eagle said. "The trail switches back, but the climb is steady. We can stop if any of you need to."

"I need to," Stuart said.

"Stu, we've barely started!" Avery said.

"Well, I do."

"Okay, let's stop if anyone *really* needs to," Phil said.

"I *really* need to!" Stuart said.

Phil sighed. "Fine." He lifted his head. "Seeking Eagle, Stuart needs to stop!"

Everyone stopped and looked at Stuart, who leaned against a tree and mopped at his streaming face with the sleeve of his shirt.

Seeking Eagle smiled. "This is good for you, brother," he said.

"So everyone tries to tell me," Stuart panted. "I'm not seeing the benefit right now."

Seeking Eagle's smile widened. "You will," he said. He looked at the others. "Ready?" He started forward again.

Stuart groaned and looked at the tall, straight back leading them. "How old do you think he is?" he asked Phil quietly, pointing at the elderly man with his chin.

"Hard to say," Phil said. "But I think we can guess he's older than any of our parents."

"And still he keeps walking!" Stuart said.

"Yup. He's certainly in good shape!" Phil said, smiling.

"Ugh!" Stuart said.

For two hours, the group alternately toiled steadily upward or collapsed against trees and drained water bottles.

"You know, I'm glad we're down here in the trees," Avery said during one of their breaks. "That sun is hot today!"

"But it's not making the climb any easier," Stuart said.

"Actually, it would be much worse out in the hot sun," Seeking Eagle said. He looked around, placing a gentle hand on an enormous spruce. "The trees are our friends."

"Well, I wish they'd help a bit more," Stuart said, twisting the lid off another water bottle.

Seeking Eagle laughed. "They are helping all they can," he said. "They are giving us shade and pure air."

Phil took a deep breath of the spicy air. "And doing a great job of it," he said.

The group trudged on.

"Wait!" Hanna said suddenly. "What is that?!"

Everyone turned and followed her pointing finger. A large, shadowy figure was slipping off through the trees.

"A bear?!" Jessie shrieked, scurrying to Seeking Eagle's side.

"It is not a bear," Seeking Eagle said. "It is a friend."

"Yours or mine?" Stuart asked shakily.

"Ours," Seeking Eagle said. "It is a . . . moose." He stared off into the thick trees for a moment. "He is here to help."

"Like the *trees* are helping?" Stuart asked. "Or some real help?"

"We shall see," Seeking Eagle said. "Come, let us continue on."

Finally, the trail opened into a wide expanse and the trees thinned out to mere patches here and there. Much of the remaining slope was covered with loose rock.

"Wow," Avery said. "This place always amazes me!"

"We will rest for a while," Seeking Eagle said. "Before we move on."

"What?!" Stuart said. "We're not staying here?"

Seeking Eagle smiled and shook his head. "No, brother, the place we seek is up there." He pointed. "Just below the false summit."

Stuart groaned and slumped down on a nearby rock.

"We should eat something," Seeking Eagle said, taking a seat on another rock.

They needed no more encouragement. Bars and fruit appeared.

And disappeared.

Finally, Seeking Eagle stood up and stretched. "It is time," he said. "You will probably need your jackets now."

Everyone packed away wrappers and containers and pulled wrinkled jackets or hoodies out of their backpacks.

"Ready," Avery said, doing up her zipper.

"*You're* ready," Stuart said.

"Come, Stuart, brother. You can help me lead." Stuart sighed and joined Seeking Eagle at the front of the group.

Together, they made their way off to the right and began the long hike up the ridge to the false summit.

"Everyone watch your steps here," Seeking Eagle said. "The loose rocks can be quite treacherous."

"Look!" Hanna pointed back behind them. "There's another moose!"

Everyone turned.

The huge animal was standing quietly at the exact spot where they had stopped to rest and eat. It was looking up at them.

"It is the same moose," Seeking Eagle said quietly.

"How do you know?" Hanna asked.

"I know. Come my brothers and sisters, let us continue."

"Hey!" There was the sound of sliding rocks.

Avery spun around to see Phil scrambling for a foothold in the loose rocks. After a few tense seconds, he was finally able to regain his balance. "Man! That scared me!" he said.

"Please be careful," Seeking Eagle said. "I would hate to have any of you injured."

"I was fine till that little animal ran across in front of me," Phil said.

"What animal?" Avery asked.

Phil looked around. "There! That one sitting on the rock."

A small animal with soft gray fur, large round ears and black eyes was looking at them.

"It's a Pika!" Avery said. "Oh, he's so cute!"

"Not so cute when they're making someone fall off a mountain!" Phil said.

"Look. There's another one!" Hanna said. "Oh, don't you just want to take one home!"

"No," Phil said grumpily. "I don't! In fact I don't care if I ever see one again!"

Avery laughed. "Oh, Phil, you're going to *hate* what I got you for your birthday!"

Phil stared at her. "You didn't . . ."

Everyone laughed.

"Let's move on my brothers and sisters," Seeking Eagle said. "We are almost there."

The elderly man continued steadily up the ridge, keeping his steps slow and careful. The kids straggled along behind him, pausing only occasionally to take in the breath-taking view.

Finally, at a crease in the natural rock, Seeking Eagle stopped. "This is where we turn," he said.

"Turn?" Avery stopped beside him and looked down. A long, sharp slope, covered almost completely in loose rocks dropped into a stone basin in the wall of the mountain. "Are we going down there?" she asked.

"Yes," Seeking Eagle said. "And we must be cautious."

The rest of the group had joined them and everyone looked down. "It looks like a basin," Hanna said. "See? The water comes from up there and pours down into it."

"That is exactly what happens," Seeking Eagle said. "When the snows melt, they form a stream that fills the basin." He pointed. "Then the water must leak out through a fissure or crack in the far wall." He pulled off his backpack. "When this spring's heavy waters rushed through, they flushed out many things. Things that had been buried since the dawn of time." He smiled at the kids. "And that is what we're here to find," he said.

"Are we all going?" Avery asked. "It looks so tiny!"

"It is larger than it appears," Seeking Eagle said. "We could easily fit all of you and several more in there." He opened his backpack and pulled out several lengths of rope. "And now, we will get to work."

Stuart moved closer. "If someone held the rope and braced their feet here and here," he indicated, "they could act as an anchor and it would make the drop easier," he said. "They really won't be holding anyone's total weight, so one person could do it."

Seeking Eagle looked and nodded. "A very good idea, Stuart," he said.

"Here, I know the knots," Stuart said. "Let me."

Seeking Eagle smiled and handed the rope to Stuart, who deftly coiled it around himself and knotted it. Then he threw the rest of the rope down the slope. It dropped to the bottom.

"How . . .?" Jessie began.

"Books," Phil said.

"Oh, right."

"Okay, now we can lower one person at a time," Stuart said.

"Two of you will remain," Seeking Eagle said. "For emergency if needed."

"Well, I'm here to stay," Stuart said. He looked down the steep slope and grinned. "You couldn't talk me into trying that!"

"Oh that just fills me with confidence!" Avery said.

Seeking Eagle smiled. "And I would like Hanna to remain, too."

Hanna nodded. "No problem," she said, moving closer to Stuart.

"The rest of us will go down one at a time," Seeking Eagle said as he stuffed most of the ropes back into his backpack and pulled it on once more. "I will go first so I can help those who follow." Deftly, he grabbed the rope and gave it a pull.

Stuart braced his feet against some large rocks and nodded.

Seeking Eagle began to back down the slope.

His steps were sure and light as he scrambled down over the loose rock. In no time he had reached the bottom.

"Okay!" he shouted. "Send down the next!"

Phil grabbed the rope and began his descent. The rocks slid and shifted beneath him, but he managed to keep his footing and was soon standing beside Seeking Eagle. "Hey, that wasn't so bad!" he said. "Come on, girls! Show us how it's done!"

Jessie started down. She moved much more carefully than either Phil or Seeking Eagle, but still managed to fall twice. Avery could see her friend's face twist with pain after the second time.

"Are you all right?" she hollered.

Seeking Eagle knelt down to examine Jessie's knee, then waved at Avery. "She is all right," he said. "Come on down!"

Avery hitched up her backpack and reached out and clutched the rope tightly. Then she turned around and started to back down the slope. "Step. Step," she repeated softly under her breath, her eyes glued to the rocks beneath her. "Step. Step."

Suddenly, she felt someone touch her back. Startled, she looked up. Phil had reached out to brace her. She was standing at the bottom. She dropped the rope and waved to Stuart and Hanna, who waved back. Then she turned to Jessie. "Are you all right?" she asked.

Jessie was clutching her knee and looking a little white, but she nodded. "It's only a bump," she said.

"She banged her knee when she fell the second time," Phil said. "But it's not even bruised, Seeking Eagle says. Painful, but not serious."

"You've got the painful part right," Jessie said, grinning.

"You rest here, my sister," Seeking Eagle said. "We will do what must be done."

"And what is that?" Avery asked.

"I don't know," Seeking Eagle said. "I know only that the Great Spirit wanted us here. In this spot. The rest is up to Him."

Avery looked at Phil and shrugged. "Well, we might as well look around," she said.

The two of them began to make their cautious way around the edge of the bowl. They had gone about half way when Jessie suddenly said," Hey. Look at that!"

They turned. She was pointing to a spot directly across from where they stood. "What is it?" Phil asked.

"I don't know," Jessie said. "A cave or something."

Now Avery could see it. A dark smear on the far wall. She started across, still moving carefully in the scree. Finally, she and Phil were standing before a crevasse in the stone. Just large enough for someone small and slight to slip through.

Avery looked at Phil. "What do you think?"

"I think that is where we need to go," Seeking Eagle said. Avery turned. The elderly man had risen and followed them soundlessly across the stones. He looked at her. "Have you the courage?"

Avery felt her heart speed up. She lifted her chin. "It is for the animals," she said.

"Good girl," Seeking Eagle put a hand on her shoulder. "You will be watched over." He looked at

[66]

Jessie. "I'm afraid we must ask you to join us, sister," he said. "You will be our ears."

Jessie nodded and got to her feet. Then she made her way slowly across the basin.

"Sit there, next to the fissure," Seeking Eagle said. Jessie sat down and leaned against the wall next to the opening.

Avery poked her head inside and tried to see. "There seems to be a light somewhere in there," she said. "Down below."

"Must be the opening I described," Seeking Eagle said. He pulled off his backpack once more and dug out the ropes and a couple of head lamps.

Avery slipped one of the lights over her head and adjusted the beam.

"That will definitely make your job easier," Seeking Eagle said, smiling. He looped the rope around Avery's slender body and knotted it. Then he pulled on it. "How does that feel?"

Avery adjusted the rope under her arms. "Not too bad," she said.

"Now when you get inside, I want you to brace your hands and feet against the wall," Seeking Eagle said. "Sort of like a spider or a bug."

"Ewww. Spider? Bug?"

Seeking Eagle smiled. "Do not worry, sister," he said. "They will not harm you."

Avery sighed. "I'm ready," she said.

"Are you sure you want to try this?" Phil said. "I could go."

"Thanks, Phil, but I think you're too big for that opening," Avery said.

Phil looked at it and scowled. "You're probably right."

"And it will take both of you to bring me back out."

"Hadn't thought of that," Phil said.

"Here," Seeking Eagle said. "I want you to take my backpack."

Avery looked at the large bag and frowned. "Why?"

"It is bigger than yours," the elderly man said. "And it is important."

"Oh. Okay." Avery slipped into the straps and adjusted them. "I'm ready." She stepped close to the fissure and leaned forward.

Seeking Eagle grabbed the rope and looped it around himself. Phil did the same. The two of them sat down and braced themselves as well as they could. Working together, they began to pay out the rope.

Avery slid into the shadow of the crevasse and braced her hands and then her feet against the rough walls. She pointed her headlamp downwards and moved her head about, trying to get a good look. "It sure goes down a long way," she said. She laughed nervously. "It looks sort of like a chimney. I feel like Santa Claus!"

"Here we go, Santa!" Seeking Eagle's voice sounded muted and strange here inside the fissure. "We will lower you slowly. You shout if you have any problems or see anything. Jessie will hear you."

"Okay!" Avery said. She began to 'walk' down the wall.

Chapter Ten

It was much easier than Avery had thought it would be. "Hey! This is fun!" she said.

"Are you okay?" Jessie's voice reached her clearly.

"Fine!" she shouted.

The chimney of stone was very rough and she had no trouble finding hand and foot-holds as she descended. Her little lamp was bright and kept the darkness back.

Slowly, she descended.

"Anything?" Jessie's voice was growing fainter.

"Not yet!" Suddenly, Avery noticed that the chimney seemed to be getting brighter. She braced her feet and, reaching up, switched off her lamp. She could still see quite clearly. Then she noticed a beam of sunlight shining on the wall below her. Carefully, she moved further down and discovered a long crack in the outer wall. She put her fingers into it and could feel a soft breeze against them. "There's a crack here," she said. "I can see sunlight!"

"Careful!" Jessie said.

Avery continued to step down the wall. But now, when she moved her feet, she could feel the wall crumble a little under her boots. She looked down and was startled to realize that the floor of the chimney was just a few feet further. Finally, her feet sank into soft dirt. She braced herself carefully and stood up. "I'm at the bottom!" she shouted.

"Good!" Jessie's voice was very faint.

It was quite bright down here. The sunlight from the crack in the wall just above her head shone at an angle on the inner surface and lit up the whole area.

Avery smiled. In the very bottom of the chimney, a yellow flower was blooming happily. She shook her head. Even here, in the bottom of a cave, flowers could grow.

But then it was so bright.

Really bright.

Avery frowned and stared at the wall. The light was shining on something in the wall. Something that reflected the light and made it even brighter. She moved closer.

Some months earlier, a prospector had visited their grade eight class, bringing with him his greatest treasure. A small gold nugget. He had passed it around the class and almost created a stampede when he had told the kids he had found it very near Banff townsite.

Nearly every student had been suddenly and violently infected with gold fever. It had taken the teacher nearly ten minutes to calm them down.

For the next month, prospecting for gold had been the major topic of conversation among her classmates. Several of them had tried to discover where the prospector had his claim, but had failed utterly.

Finally, when no one had seen the least success, gold fever had changed to gold interest. Then had been forgotten altogether.

Now, Avery felt that same stirring of excitement. That same breathless anticipation.

Because there before her was a huge chunk of gold.

A huge chunk.

Embedded in the wall.

Avery stared. It must have been washed free during the flood at spring thaw.

[70]

She looked down. Lying in the dirt under her feet were several more pieces of the precious mineral. Rough and dirty, but still recognizable. She bent down and picked up a couple. It was definitely gold.

Avery's mind was suddenly leaping with thoughts of bags of cash, deluxe animal accommodations and scores of happy tourists.

She leaned her head back and shouted," I've found something!"

"Are you ready to come up?" Jessie's voice was faint but still quite clear.

"Not yet!"

Quickly now, she tore off her back pack and began stuffing in every bit of the precious metal she could find. She scrambled around in the dirt and unearthed several large pieces. Then she turned to the chunk still embedded in the wall.

How could she get it out? She opened the backpack and started hunting through it for something – a tool – to use to pry the gold from the wall. Her hand touched something cold and hard. She pulled it out.

A knife. In a stiff, leather sheath.

Quickly, she pulled the knife from its case and stabbed the point of it into the wall just beside the gold.

Some of the stone chipped off. She jabbed again and again.

Slowly, she worked her way around the visible signs of the gold. Suddenly, Avery jumped to one side as an enormous piece of the rock wall broke off and fell at her feet, taking the gold with it. It broke into several pieces when it landed. She moved back to the space where it had been and carefully examined the spot, but there was no further sign of the precious metal. Finally, she knelt down and sorted

[71]

through the pieces, rolling those containing gold into her backpack and fastening it carefully. Then she sifted through the dirt for any other pieces she might have missed.

And that's when the floor moved beneath her.

"Avery! Something's wrong!" Jessie's voice came down clearly. "We have to bring you back up!"

Avery felt the rope tighten under her arms, pulling her upright. "No! Wait!" she screamed. She struggled to touch Seeking Eagle's backpack.

It was just out of reach.

Breathing heavily, she bent and strained. "Stop! Stop!" she shouted. But, slowly, she moved further away.

She felt the walls shiver around her. From somewhere, she heard a low, grinding rumble. It grew louder and louder.

Desperately she swung her foot one last time at the backpack and almost sobbed with relief when her boot snagged one of the straps. She pushed her other boot through the strap and struggled to lift her feet toward her without losing the heavy backpack and its precious cargo.

The roar was building around her but she ignored it as she lifted her feet carefully. Finally, she managed to get them high enough that she was able to grab the strap with one hand. She gripped it with everything she had.

And it was at that moment that the walls around her . . . disappeared. Sliding past her in a blur and a cloud of choking dust with a roar that sounded like a freight train.

A piece of stone hit her in the back of the head and she felt the slow, warm trickle of blood down her back. Another large chunk bounced off her left shoulder and her hand went numb.

And then the sun was shining into her eyes and Avery was free, dangling in midair above the upper slope of the amphitheater, bruised and bleeding, but alive.

And that was when she realized that she had lost the backpack.

"Noooo!" she moaned. She felt as though her heart had dropped into her boots. Slow tears started to course down her face.

Avery felt the rope tighten and slowly, slowly, she began to move upward once more. Finally, she could see Jessie's worried face, peering over the cliff at her. She wiped her eyes and waved weakly, then saw Jessie droop with relief. "She's alive!" She heard Jessie say.

And then Phil and Seeking Eagle were pulling her over the edge and away from the cliff face.

"I'm all right," Avery said. "I bumped my shoulder and cut my head, but I'm all right." She looked at Seeking Eagle. "I lost the backpack. I lost the gold." Then she burst into tears.

Seeking Eagle put an arm around her, handed her a clean handkerchief and let her cry. With gentle fingers, he tilted her head forward slightly and said something Avery couldn't quite hear. Then she felt a soft cloth being pressed against the back of her head.

Jessie and Phil's voices overlapped each other. "I was so scared!" Phil was saying. "I thought we had lost you! All we could do was hang on!"

"It's a good thing there were two of them!" Jessie was saying at the same time. "When that wall slid off! One person never could have held you!"

Avery wiped her eyes and glanced over to where the tall chimney of rock had been.

Had been.

There wasn't even a hint of it left. Only the sheer edge of the cliff face sitting stark and bare. Avery sighed. All of her hopes had disappeared with the tons of rock.

She felt a fresh flood of tears as she shivered and turned away. It was then she saw the deep grooves in the soil, made by the boots of Seeking Eagle and Phil as they tried desperately to brace themselves and hold onto her. Phil's anxious face came into view. "Thank you," she said to him. Then she patted the rough, elderly hand that was holding the cloth to her wound. "Thank you both."

* * *

The next few minutes were a blur. Seeking Eagle insisted on carrying Avery to the top of the ridge. Phil followed closely behind, supporting Jessie and ready to help if Seeking Eagle needed it, but the elderly man seemed to have no trouble.

And Stuart and Hanna roped themselves together and handled the weight of all of them with ease.

Finally, their group was, once again, seated at the top of the ridge. For a moment, they simply sat, breathing and thinking about what had just happened.

What could have happened.

Avery dropped her head into her hands. "I had it," she moaned. "I had it all!" She looked up at them, tears making tracks on her dusty cheeks. "Enough to build our animal sanctuary."

"Enough of what?" Jessie was peering into her face.

"Gold."

"Gold?" Stuart crouched beside her.

Avery nodded. "A chunk so big." She held out her hands. "It could have built our sanctuary and I

[74]

wasn't . . . strong . . . enough . . ." She gulped and new tears started.

The others moved closer and patted her gently on the back.

Hanna took a deep breath. "Well, you may have had the gold for a moment," she said practically, "but *you* are more important!"

She was right. The gold may have helped them, but Avery's escape had been a real and very near thing. It needed to remain foremost in their minds.

And then, a moose appeared, towering over them with his huge antlers, long nose and great, brown eyes.

For a moment, they stared at him. Then Seeking Eagle scrambled to his feet and bowed slightly.

Everyone heard the 'conversation' between the two.

First, the moose. "*Trouble?*"

Seeking Eagle pointed at Avery, then at Jessie. "*They have been injured.*"

"*I will help.*"

And Avery, with Jessie clinging to her tightly, found herself coming down off the mountain riding a moose. Of all the strange things that had happened that day, this was the strangest.

But once they reached the relatively level ground of the amphitheater, the moose made a wide turn.

In the wrong direction.

"Where are you going?!" Avery asked. She looked at Seeking Eagle. "Where is he going?"

Seeking Eagle just shook his head. "I don't know, my sister," he said. "But it is best to let him do what he must."

"But he's leading us in the wrong direction!" Avery said. Her head was beginning to hurt, and a million little cuts and bruises she hadn't noticed before.

"The Great Spirit leads me."

"What?" Avery looked down at the stiff, brown hair beneath her hands, then to the giant antlers just in front of her. "What did you say?"

The moose turned his great head slightly and looked back at her and Jessie. She could almost hear the smile in the next 'words'. *"The Great Spirit leads us all."*

Avery stared at her mount. *"Umm. Okay,"* she said at last.

The moose made his way toward a huge pile of rubble near the back of the amphitheater. Finally, he stopped at the edge of what must have been, only a few minutes before, Avery's chimney of rock.

Avery and Jessie slid, rather stiffly, from the tall, boney back. The others joined them.

They all heard the moose quite clearly. *"Here. This is what you seek."*

Avery looked out over the great pile of broken rock and sighed. Some pieces were bigger than she was.

She sighed. "We'll never find that backpack," she said mournfully.

"Never say never!" Phil said, darting forward onto the rocks and teetering along, windmilling his arms wildly to keep his balance. Suddenly, he whooped, stopped and bent down, then emerged triumphantly holding what was left of the backpack.

"You found it!" Avery said excitedly. "Quick! Bring it here!"

Phil shook his head and stuck one hand through the bag. The entire bottom had been ripped away. Whatever the bag had once held was long gone.

Avery slumped down onto the ground, again feeling near to tears. She had been so close! All of her dreams had slipped, quite literally, through her fingers.

"Sorry, Ave," Phil said. "I . . ." Then he stopped and bent down. "Hey!" he shouted. "Come over here!"

The rest of the group made their way as quickly as possible across the rocks to where Phil was kneeling.

Heart thumping wildly and aching head forgotten, Avery followed the rest as quickly as she could.

By the time she had reached the group, all of them were digging frantically through the rocks, pulling out lumps of . . . gold?

"You found it!" Avery said.

Seeking Eagle looked at her. "This is what was in that chimney of rock," he said.

"Yes," Avery said. "Most of it was lying on the bottom, but some was still stuck in the wall."

"Stuck in the wall?" Seeking Eagle frowned thoughtfully.

She nodded.

"And you got it out?"

"I found a knife in your backpack and chipped it out," Avery said.

Seeking Eagle looked thoughtful. "Perhaps that is why the walls . . ."

"Collapsed," Avery said sadly. "Yeah, I pretty much figured that out already."

The group had already found quite a pile of dully-shining, lumps of gold.

"Wow!" Avery said. She frowned. "I'm sure this is way more than I had in the backpack."

Seeking Eagle smiled. "There are many ways that the Great Spirit helps us. Usually after we have done all we can." His smile widened. "And when things look the blackest."

The group toiled away, collecting nuggets and rocks and adding them to the growing pile.

"Oh, now I know this is more than I had before!" she said.

Seeking Eagle smiled again.

Finally, he sat back and wiped his forehead with a dusty hand and looked up at the sky. "Perhaps we had better quit for the day," he said. "The darkness will catch us on our way down the mountain."

"But how can we leave?" Stuart asked. "What if someone comes up here and steals our gold?"

Seeking Eagled looked at him. "It is given to us by the Great Spirit for a specific purpose," he said. "Do you think He cannot protect what is His?"

Stuart sighed. "I guess so," he said, uncertainly.

"Do not worry, my brother. The gold is ours for our needs," Seeking Eagle said. "The Great Spirit will look after it."

"I still think we should carry as much of it with us as we can," Stuart said. "And cover up what we can't manage."

"Of course!" Seeking Eagle agreed.

Each of them stuffed as much as they could carry into their packs and struggled to their feet.

"Good thing it's mostly downhill from here," Phil said.

They poured dirt over the remaining rocks, disguising their true nature.

"Okay, we're ready," Hanna said.

Seeking Eagle helped Avery, then Jessie climb up on the tall moose once more.

Then they started down.

* * *

The sun was setting over the far side of the mountain. Already, it was growing difficult to see in the long shadows beneath the trees.

"Can we stop for a moment?" Hanna asked. "I'm getting so tired!"

The moose stopped and looked around at her. "*Help*?"

Hanna looked at it gratefully. "*Oh yes, please!*"

"*Give me your packs.*"

Phil produced a couple of lengths of rope and lashed two backpacks together. Then he and Seeking Eagle draped them over the back of the giant animal in front of Avery.

"All set?" Seeking Eagle asked. "We need to keep moving."

With most of the heavy packs being carried by the moose, and the last one being shared between Stuart, Phil and Seeking Eagle, they made quick progress and, in a short time, were once again crossing the grassy ski slopes beneath the chair lifts.

Avery looked up at them. "Seems like a lifetime ago that we were here," she said.

The others nodded wearily.

The moose left them beside the Mount Norquay parking lot and trundled away back through the trees. "Thank you, brother!" Seeking Eagle called after him.

The moose turned and gave them a long look. Then nodded and continued on his way.

Everyone slumped down, tired and bruised, but happy, into the grass.

Phil pulled out his cell phone and dialed. "Mom? We're back at the parking lot," he said. He listened for a moment. "Okay," he said. "See you soon!" He slid the phone back into his pocket. "She'll be here in a few minutes."

"Well, as long as we have a while to wait," Avery said. "Let's talk about how we're going to get the rest of the gold."

Seeking Eagle smiled and nodded.

"We'll just have to keep going back every day and carrying down what we can," Stuart said. "Maybe bring a wagon or something that can handle those trails."

"I have an old wagon," Avery said. "From when I was little. A really sturdy one!"

"I do not know if a wagon will be possible," Seeking Eagle said. He frowned thoughtfully. "I will tell you what," he went on. "I will think on this. I may have an answer."

Everyone agreed. No one had the energy to offer another solution.

For a few minutes, they were silent, lost in their own thoughts.

"I think I know what all of you are thinking," Stuart said, finally. "That we're all rich!"

Avery looked at him and smiled. "Aren't you forgetting something?" she asked.

Stuart frowned. "Forgetting something?" he said.

"Who directed us to that spot?" Avery asked. "Who told us where to look when we asked for help for the animals?"

"Ummm . . ." Stuart said.

"This gold was given to us to help the animals, Stuart," Avery said, holding up one of the smaller nuggets from her backpack. "It is for them."

"But . . ." Stuart said.

"Would we have found it any other way?"

"Well . . . no," Stuart said.

"Right." Avery threw her nugget back into her pack. "Discussion over." She frowned. "So," she added. "Does anyone know what do with gold?"

Chapter Eleven

"And then we – ouch! – climbed down into the bowl – ouch! – and I crawled into a little cave – ouch! – and that's when I found the . . ." Avery broke off and twisted slightly to eye the doctor. She was lying facedown on the table in the hospital emergency room, while he prodded and cleaned.

Her concerned parents were sitting on chairs on the far side of the room.

"I won't have to get my head shaved, will I?" she asked suddenly.

"What?" the doctor stopped what he was doing and looked at her.

"My hair. I won't have to get it shaved off, will I?"

"Why would I do that?" the doctor was back cleaning again.

"Well, I thought – ouch! – that if you had to sew me up – ouch! – that you'd have to shave my head first."

The doctor laughed and tossed a red-stained piece of cloth into a bowl of antiseptic. "The cut isn't deep enough to need stitches," he said. He straightened and looked at her parents. "Your daughter has been pretty shaken up," he said, "but I see no cause for alarm at this time." He helped Avery sit up. "I'd keep an eye on her for possible signs of concussion – sleepiness, nausea. But I really don't think you have much to worry about."

Avery's mom came over, leaned against the bed and put an arm around her daughter. "I'm so glad," she said. "That must have been quite a fall you took!"

"Yeah," Avery said, not meeting her mother's eyes. "Well, there was a lot of loose rock around."

"I do have another concern," the doctor said. He pulled up the back of Avery's shirt, disclosing bright red marks that wrapped around her chest and continued up behind her shoulders. "These."

Her parents stared at them. "Umm . . . Avery," her dad said, "Do you want to tell us anything?"

Avery sighed. "It's nothing, Dad, really," she said, pulling her shirt down. "Seeking Eagle and Phil put a rope around me when I was going down . . . the slope. So I hopefully wouldn't do what I did."

"But honey . . ." her mom began.

"Can we talk about this later?" Avery asked.

Her dad looked at the doctor, who nodded.

"As far as I'm concerned, she's good to go home," the doctor said. "I'd put some salve on those friction burns and keep an eye on her mental state. But she should be just fine." He smiled at Avery. "Just be a bit more careful when you're hiking," he said. He smiled and left them.

"So what did you find that you didn't want the doctor to hear about?" her dad asked.

"You heard that, did you?" Avery said.

"Hard to miss!" her mom said. "So . . .?"

Avery leaned toward them. "Gold!" she whispered.

Her parents stared at her. "Gold?!"

"Shhh! We don't want anyone else to hear about it until we get it assayed and sold!" Avery said.

"But . . . but . . ." her mom began.

"I'll tell you all about it when we get home," Avery said. She looked around. "Less chance of anyone overhearing us there."

Her parents frowned, but agreed.

"Right!" Avery slipped to her feet. "Let's go!" Her parents followed her out into the hospital waiting room.

"Avery!" Hanna said, as her friends jumped to their feet and crowded around her. She grinned. At least she though they were her friends. All of them were sweat-streaked and liberally coated in dust.

"What did the doctor say?" Phil asked.

"He says I'm fine," Avery said. "But not to be so clumsy when I'm hiking."

"Oh," Hanna said, eyeing Avery's parents.

Seeking Eagle pushed through. "It is my fault," he said quietly. "I am to blame!"

"No one's to blame!" Avery's dad said. "It's hiking. These things happen!"

"I appreciate your kindness," Seeking Eagle said, bowing his head slightly. "I did not mean for this to happen."

"Oh, don't worry about it," Avery's mom said. "We live in the mountains. We know how hiking can be – even with the most careful people." She looked at Avery and smiled. "And let's face it; Avery isn't the most careful of people!"

"Mom!" Avery protested.

The others laughed rather weakly.

"I did not know the walls were weak, or I never would have allowed her to go."

"Oh, Seeking Eagle, there's loose rock everywhere up there!" Avery said, hurriedly. "Come on, let's go!" She started toward the doors.

"Walls?" Avery's mom said, following her. "What's he talking about?"

"Oh, he means the walls of the amphitheater," Avery said. "And we all know about the rubble up there!"

"Yes, it can certainly be treacherous," Avery's dad said.

"Right!" Avery said. "And now I want to go home. I'm tired. And hungry. And I definitely need a bath!" She waved to the rest of the group as she and her parents slid into their van. "See you guys later!"

"Is Seeking Eagle taking the gold with him?" her dad asked as he put the van into gear.

"Yes," Avery said. "He knows what to do to get it assayed and sold."

Avery's parents looked at each other. "I don't mean to sound awful, but can you trust him?" her mom asked.

"Mom, you trusted him with your daughter!" Avery said. "Now you're worried about trusting him with his own gold?"

"That did sound horrible, didn't it," her mom said, making a face.

"Besides, it isn't for any of us," Avery went on. "It's for the animals!"

"Right," her dad said. He reached out and laid a hand on his wife's leg. "It'll be just fine, honey, I promise!"

* * *

Early the next morning, Avery and her friends waited on the benches in front of the museum for Seeking Eagle. A few minutes later, he joined them, carrying several bulky bundles. "Are you ready?" he asked.

Avery grinned. "I'm stiff and sore all over," she said. "But I'm raring to go!" She got up and poked her head inside the museum. "Dad! We're ready!"

"Coming!" Her dad appeared. "You're sure you want to do this?" he asked. "I mean, it's only been a few hours since you were up there!"

Everyone nodded.

"We're sure," Avery said. She lowered her voice. "We need to get that gold out of there," she added.

Her dad nodded. "I suppose you're right," he said. He turned and led all of them to the van.

Seeking Eagle stowed his bundles and everyone climbed inside.

"Now I want you to be careful today!" Avery's dad said as he negotiated the roads to Mt. Norquay. "Or, you know, I could come up with you!"

"Don't worry, Dad," Avery said. "We don't have to go up on the cliff this time. We'll just be staying down in the amphitheater!"

"Well, good," her dad said. "And call if you need any help."

"We will," Avery said. "But I don't know if there will be any signal up there."

"There is," her dad said. "At least there is at the top of the ski slopes."

"We will be fine," Seeking Eagle said. "We have many friends who will be helping us today."

"Friends?" Avery's dad turned to look at the elderly man. "Who? Anyone I know?"

"You can trust them, Michael," Seeking Eagle said, putting a gnarled hand on the younger man's sleeve. "They are true friends."

Avery's dad frowned, then sighed and shrugged. "Well, I'll take your word for it," he said. "Okay." He stopped at the far side of the parking lot. "Be careful!" he said again.

"We'll be fine, dad!" Avery said. "Love you!"

He smiled. "Love you, too, honey," he said.

Seeking Eagle grabbed the bundles he had stowed in the back of the van and handed one to each of the kids. Then he started along the now-familiar path with the others falling into step behind him.

This time, with the promise of excitement before them, the hike to the amphitheater didn't seem so long.

"Wait!" Phil said as they came out of the trees. "There's a herd of . . ." he squinted, ". . . moose. Huh. That's strange. Moose don't travel in herds! Well, we'd better wait for them to move on."

Seeking Eagle smiled and started across the amphitheater. "They are friends, my brother," he said. "Here to help us!"

One of the huge animals came out to meet them and Avery thought she recognized the same moose who had helped them the day before.

"We are ready, my brothers and I."

Seeking Eagle bowed slightly. *"I thank you all."*

"It is no trouble."

As the other moose gathered quietly around, Seeking Eagle unrolled his bundle, revealing long, canvas sacks, tied together in pairs. These were, in turn, attached to a thick, leather belt, complete with a buckle. He threw one of the contraptions across the tall back of the animal nearest to him, fastening and adjusting the belt so that it protected the moose's back and held the sacks in place, one on each side.

"There," he said. "What do you think?"

"Oh, I get it," Stuart said. "These animals will be carrying the gold down the mountain for us!"

"Exactly!" Seeking Eagle said, grinning.

The elderly man's plan worked beautifully.

For the next two hours, they all worked in two teams. Stuart, Phil and Seeking Eagle sifted through the rubble, extracting any gold they could find. Avery, Hanna and Jessie dropped them into the canvas sacks strapped to their ever-patient 'pack mules'.

Finally, Seeking Eagle straightened and stretched. "I think we've found about all we're going

[87]

to find," he said. "Further searching will require equipment and skills none of us have."

"Thank goodness!" Jessie said. "I'm tired!"

"As am I!" Hanna said.

"How much do you think we've found?" Stuart asked.

"Well, I think we've strapped about two hundred pounds onto each of ten animals," Seeking Eagle said. "That's about a ton of rock."

"Wow! That would have taken us a month to carry down in backpacks!" Jessie said.

"It makes me tired just thinking about it!" Hanna said.

"You! What about me!" Stuart moaned.

"Shall we go?" Seeking Eagle asked. He started across the amphitheater toward the forest on the far side. The kids fell into step behind him and the line of moose brought up the rear.

After a few minutes, Avery stopped and looked around. "Okay, this is the strangest thing I've ever seen," she said. "I know I keep thinking that, but this time, it's true!"

The others stopped and glanced behind them at the procession of heavily-laden moose.

"I think I agree with you," Phil said.

The trip back down the mountain went very quickly. The hikers, with virtually empty backpacks, practically skipped along. And the moose, though they appeared large and ungainly, were quite agile. Even carrying two large, heavy sacks each.

When they finally reached the parking lot, Seeking Eagle kept walking. "We will have to walk right to the bottom," he said.

Stuart groaned.

"It's only about six kilometers, nature boy!" Avery said. "And it's all downhill!"

Stuart shook his head. "I don't know why anyone would want to do this for fun!"

"Come on, Stu, admit it," Phil said. "You've had fun today!"

"I'm admitting nothing," Stuart said, putting his nose into the air, then tripping on a rock in the road.

"I'd like to admit something!" Jessie said.

Everyone laughed.

The road, with its switchbacks, made the downward hike easy. Soon, they were crossing the bridge over the Trans Canada highway.

"Everyone's looking at us!" Phil said.

Avery turned her head. Cars below them were slowing, obviously to get a glimpse of the train of pack-moose crossing the bridge. "Yep. I guess this is something *they* don't see every day, either," she said, grinning.

"Or ever!" Phil added.

When they reached the townsite, Seeking Eagle stopped. "Our friends and I will take the gold to be sold," he said. "I will leave you now."

"Thank you, Seeking Eagle," Avery said. "If it weren't for you, none of this would have happened!"

The elderly man smiled and bowed his head. "The Great Spirit commands," he said simply. "And I obey!"

The kids watched as he turned and went the opposite direction, with the moose falling into step behind him.

"Well, that was a day I'll never forget!" Stuart said as the five friends started walking.

"Memorable for so many reasons!" Jessie said. "Like you climbing a mountain!"

"For the second time!" Hanna said.

Stuart made a face. "I think I could get used to it," he said.

"If there's gold at the top!" Phil said.

"Shhh!" Avery said. "Don't let anyone hear you!"

"Avery, what can they do?" Stuart said.

"I don't know," Avery said. "And I don't want to find out! Now let's hurry, because I'm hungry!"

* * *

Anxious to tell her friends what they had discovered, Avery hurried to the museum the next morning.

She pulled the door open and for a moment, paused to gaze around. How different it all was, with the birds, insects and animals everywhere but *inside* their display cases. She looked up at the golden light pouring through the upper lantern windows and reflected on the fine, cross-cut logs that formed the walls. It really was a beautiful building.

She grinned. But now, maybe the animals would have a *real* home!

Hehaka looked over the upper bannister at her, then began to make his way to the first floor.

Avery moved carefully across the packed main floor towards him.

The two of them met at the bottom of the stairs.

The huge animal looked at her. *"You have news?"*

"I do! My friends and I were directed to a place where we found gold! We might be able to build your home now!"

The great bull nodded his head. *"It is good."*

Avery smiled at him, then at the other birds, animals and insects that had gathered around the two of them. *"Did you hear? We can maybe build your new home!"*

Everyone around her began to jump and shuffle, bumping into each other in their excitement.

Avery laughed and looked over them all. Her friends. She glanced upward, taking in the eager faces of the animals on the stairs and the second floor. The she let her gaze wander even higher, toward the animals on the wall beneath the great lantern windows.

All of the heads inside the lantern were moving around, flapping their ears and looking at each other, obviously infected by the good news.

All of them.

Avery stared at the one head of the eight hanging there.

The one head that, until now, had been lifeless and inert.

It, too was moving. As she watched, it turned toward her and . . . closed one eye in a slow, deliberate wink.

Just then, Avery heard the front door open. She glanced over her shoulder to see Seeking Eagle step inside.

She went over to him. "The moose is alive," she said.

Seeking Eagle smiled at her.

"The one up there!" Avery pointed.

Seeking Eagled followed her finger. "Yes," he said.

"Is that all you can say?" Avery asked. She narrowed her eyes. "It's the same moose, isn't it?"

Seeking Eagle's smile widened.

"I know it's the same moose that brought Jess and I down from the mountain! And that collected his friends . . ." the realization hit her, ". . . those others were real moose, weren't they? Real, *live* moose."

Seeking Eagle smiled again, but simply said, "They were friends of the Spirit."

Avery shook her head and returned his smile. "Definitely friends!" she said. "Oh, by the way, the animals are all excited about possibly moving into their new place."

"You told them?"

She nodded. "Just a moment ago."

"Ah," Seeking Eagle said. "I was going to wait until we knew what we had."

"And do you know now?" Avery said eagerly.

"Well, let me put it this way," Seeking Eagle said. "We will definitely have enough for their building!"

* * *

Her dad choked on a bite of spaghetti and meatballs. "How much?!"

"Well, according to Seeking Eagle, the gold is worth nearly six million dollars," Avery said.

"*Six million!*"

"What are we talking about in here?" Avery's mom said as she took her seat at the table. "Oh, hon, do you want some more salad?" She handed the bowl she was carrying to her husband.

Avery's dad didn't respond.

"Hon?"

He turned slowly and looked at his wife. "*Six million dollars*, Maureen! *Six million!*"

Avery's mom stared at him and shook her head. "What about it?" she asked, finally.

"That is what Seeking Eagle got for the gold these kids found."

"What?!" Avery's mom set the bowl down. Hard. "*Six million?*"

"Dollars," her dad said.

"Oh my word!"

For a moment, her parents just looked at each other blankly.

"Ahem!" Avery said. "If I could interrupt for a moment?"

Both of them turned numbly and looked at her.

"This is money we raised to house and care for the animals of the museum," Avery said. "For. The. Animals."

Her dad blinked. "Oh, right," he said. "For the animals."

Her mom shook her head. "Of course," she said. "What on earth were we thinking?"

"I know what you were thinking," Avery said. "About how that money could put a new roof on our house and take care of us forever?"

Her parents laughed lightly, obviously embarrassed.

"Right. Right," her dad said.

"But the Great Spirit spoke to Seeking Eagle and told him where to look. We never would have found it if it weren't for that! That money is for the animals!"

"Of course, dear," her mom said, heaving a great sigh. "Of course."

Her dad sat back in his chair. "Just think of what that money will mean," he said. "A whole new facility! Maybe a whole new museum!"

"Six million will go a long way toward making those animals comfortable," her mom said.

Her parents were fast returning to normal.

Avery heaved a sigh of relief. Her friends had reacted much the same way when Seeking Eagle had gotten them all together earlier that day. Stuart hadn't been able to speak for over a minute. Something very unusual for him.

Avery had to admit that she had even had her dreams of things she could do with that much money.

But Seeking Eagle had quietly cleared his throat and said, "Remember who gave us this money and what it is for," he said.

His words were like a pail of cold water down Avery's back. Of course!

"Well, we'll have to start planning," her dad said.

Avery grinned.

Chapter Twelve

"Oh, it's a perfect spot!" Avery said excitedly. "Perfect!"

She looked around at the trees crowding close. "And you can't even tell that the town is just over there!" She pointed with her chin.

Just then, she heard the warning scream of the train whistle. "The train is a bit close. And loud," she said, covering her ears. "But I'm sure it won't disturb anything. Or anybody!"

Her dad laughed. "So what do you think? Is this the spot to build our new zoo?"

"I think it's wonderful!" Avery said. "But it's not up to me."

Her dad frowned. "What do you mean?" He shook his head. "The wrangling we've had to endure to get this place! You know how hard it is to get permission to build in the park these days! If it hadn't been such a spectacularly strange and unique situation, your precious animals would already be setting up housekeeping in Calgary!"

Avery smiled. "I know, Dad!" she said. "I only meant that we should probably check with the creatures that will be living here."

"Oh," her dad said. Then he grinned and added, "Living. Well, that's debatable!"

"Let's go and ask them now!" Avery said, turning toward the van.

Her dad laughed and climbed behind the wheel. "Fine!" he said.

It took only a few minutes for them to cross the town and pull to a stop beside the museum.

"Huh," Avery said. "I wonder where everyone is."

The animals were noticeably absent on this bright and sunny late-summer day. Only people were visible on the lawns and grounds surrounding the museum.

"Probably inside," her dad said, grinning. "Playing poker or something like that."

Avery made a face at him and climbed out of the vehicle. Side by side, they walked across the wide patio and into the beautiful building.

"Huh. I think we've interrupted a meeting," Avery whispered to her dad.

"It certainly looks that way," he said.

Seeking Eagle had again taken up a position atop the central display cabinet. Every animal, bird and insect in the place was obviously giving him their undivided attention.

"What are they saying?" her dad asked quietly.

"Shhh, I'm trying to make it out!" Avery said. She frowned in concentration.

Finally, she looked at her father. "Seeking Eagle is explaining that we now have the approval to build them a facility right here in Banff."

The animals began to stir. Flapping. Stomping. Grunting. Bugling. Their obvious support was getting rather noisy.

"It looks as though they're okay with it," her dad said.

Avery smiled at him. "Definitely okay," she said. "Uh-oh."

"What is it?" Her dad looked worried.

"Well, he just asked if any of them wanted to see the spot," Avery said.

"And?"

"They all do," Avery said. She grinned. "This ought to be good."

"Uh-oh."

The following impromptu parade to and from, tied up traffic in the town of Banff for over two hours and nearly drove the whole RCMP constabulary crazy.

Hehaka and Seeking Eagle led the way, with every type of bird, animal and insect ever to have lived within the park boundaries following as closely as possible behind them. For most of the animals, this was their first foray past the grounds of the museum and into modern Banff, and they were understandably curious.

More than one park visitor shrieked in surprise and alarm at finding one animal or another peering into the doorways of the many shops.

Mato, especially, seemed to be enjoying himself as he stood up on his hind legs and stopped in entrance after entrance.

One woman fainted dead away.

The two great pelicans lit on one of the benches, spilling tourists onto the sidewalk. After a moment, they spread their wings and took to the air once more, leaving the people gaping after them.

Floating just above the heads of the animals and obviously enjoying himself, the great trout swam lazily, occasionally flipping his tail and sending himself leaping higher into the air. More than one spectator rubbed their eyes and pointed at the strange sight.

As the animals continued to make their way down Banff Avenue, more and more people crowded the sidewalks to watch them pass. Camera flashes grew nearly constant, and shouts of, 'Hey get me with ___' echoed over the crowd.

"Honestly, Dr. Mike!" one of the RCMP officers said as he tried to straighten out a particularly bad knot in the traffic. "Couldn't you have arranged things beforehand? Maybe planned out a route. I don't know . . . be prepared?"

Avery's dad laughed and winked at Avery. "This wasn't my doing, Ray," he said. "And, for the record, we tried to lead them down beside the river. They wouldn't do it! They wanted to cruise straight down main! These animals have minds of their own."

The officer glared at both of them, then suddenly jumped. "No, ma'am you can't leave your car there!" he bellowed. "I don't care if it *is* the picture of a lifetime!"

Avery and her dad moved quickly out of earshot.

Finally, the leaders turned the parade off Banff Avenue and down Elk Street, then to Railway Avenue and at last, onto Mt. Norquay Road. A few minutes later, they were parading past the recreation center to the spot that had been designated for their future home.

For several minutes, the animals, birds and insects continued to gather around the leaders, with the curious humans who had tagged along, forming a group behind them. Movement slowed. Then stopped. The animals gazed silently at the peaceful, pristine woods. Finally, Hehaka lifted his great head and looked at Seeking Eagle.

"It is acceptable," the elderly man said.

Everyone gathered let out a great cheer.

* * *

Avery paused as she started to open the door to the sports arena. She turned her head and looked across the parking lot at the busy building site for the future Banff zoo. From here she had a good view. The skeletal structure loomed up, its height rivaling the tall, ancient pines around it. Men in hard hats swarmed over the area, hauling materials and equipment, talking and laughing.

The building was going up so fast, it was almost magical.

Avery saw something move in the shadows to one side of the site. A herd of elk were silently watching. She stared hard at the animals, but their attention remained with the workers. Finally, they turned and disappeared into the trees.

Curious, Avery thought. All of the 'live' animals in the park seemed to be interested in everything that was going on here, too. She pushed on the door and stepped inside, then made her way quickly to 'her' arena. The animals had moved in a week before and were nicely settled.

She paused just outside and peered through the glass of the doors. The place was busy today. Animals and tourists milled about, obviously enjoying each other's company. Avery smiled as she thought about that first day only seven days before. The hesitance and natural fear of the humans. The warm friendliness of the animals. The stepping forward of one or two brave souls.

After that, it had only taken a few minutes for the people to realize that these animals weren't going to hurt them. Then the two groups had intermingled completely and joyously.

Avery smiled now, as she watched a family with three tiny kids posing with Mato for a picture. The great bear was, as usual, relishing the attention. The smallest of the kids had thrown his arms around the huge bear and nestled into his warm fur. The rest of the family was gathered around, showing huge grins to the camera.

The two other bears were mugging for yet another camera, both of them balanced on their hind feet and roaring ferociously while several teenagers cowered in mock-fear.

Off to one side, a group of children was contentedly sitting on wooden benches, holding and petting several of the smaller animals.

And one boy was completely covered in bees. He laughed and turned slowly while his family snapped pictures.

Hehaka was the center of attention. Standing in the middle of the room, he was quietly submitting to being rubbed and petted. One enterprising young man actually swung up on the narrow back and posed like a wild-west cowboy.

Hehaka caught Avery's eye and winked. Then he suddenly reared up on his hind legs and pawed the air. The boy lunged forward and wrapped both arms around the great deer's neck. There were shrieks of laughter from the surrounding tourists and the flash of dozens of cameras.

Avery laughed and started to push the door open.

A large sign fastened to it caught her attention. *"Welcome to the Banff Park Zoo"*, it said. *"Here you will find many of the birds, animals and insects who once roamed these picturesque mountains and valleys. Please treat them with respect."*

Avery smiled and stepped inside.

The noise instantly surrounded her. The sounds of the animals. The voices of many excited human beings.

"Avery! Where have you been!" Hanna was suddenly standing beside her.

"Had some homework to do," Avery said, smiling. "Looks like no one missed me anyway!"

Hanna laughed. "Well . . . it has been pretty busy!" she said.

"Avery! 'Bout time!" Jessie moved quickly through a group surrounding Heecha, the Great Horned Owl and threw an arm around Hanna. "We've barely been able to keep up!" She grinned.

Avery tipped her head to one side and looked at her two friends. Both were wearing the bright red shirts with the logo 'BARC' on the left shoulder. Avery smoothed her own, matching shirt.

"Looking spiffy, aren't we?" Jessie said.

"Always," someone said. They all turned to see Stuart approaching, with Wanbli, the great bald eagle, perched on one wrist. Heads turned as he passed and several people pointed to the great bird and spoke excitedly. He grinned. "Looks like we're a hit," he said.

"You? Or the zoo?" Avery said.

"Oh, us," Stuart said, his grin widening. "Of course us!" Wanbli turned and grabbed a lock of Stuart's hair, giving it a tug. "Hey!" Stuart looked at the great bird. "Okay, you," he said.

Wanbli fluffed his feathers and looked pleased with himself.

The girls laughed.

"Has anyone seen Phil?" Avery asked.

"Oh, yeah. He's over there," Hanna pointed. "Trying to keep the enthusiastic under control around Igmu Taka."

Avery followed her friend's pointing finger and caught sight of Phil's red shirt in the center of a tangle of tourists. Somewhere in the middle of the mob, she could just barely make out the great cougar. "Oh, poor baby," she said.

"What are you talking about?" Stuart demanded. "He loves it!"

"They all do!" Hanna said, looking around.

Avery let her eyes wander about the huge room. Everywhere, she could see the obvious excitement of the tourists. But now, she could also see how much the animals were enjoying themselves, too.

Mato had left the family to their pictures and wandered toward a crying toddler and his parents. Then the great bear flopped down on his belly on the floor in front of the little child. The boy crawled up onto the fur-covered mountain and lay down comfortably. Instantly, the two of them were surrounded by laughing, pointing tourists with their ever-present cameras. Mato looked . . . happy.

"You can't blame them," Jessie said. "According to Seeking Eagle, this opportunity is exactly what they have been waiting for. For centuries!"

"How would Seeking Eagle know they had been waiting centuries?" Avery asked.

Jessie shrugged. "I guess they told him," she said.

"Oh. Right." She looked at Mato again. "They sure do seem happy."

"Yeah, them and the tourists," Stuart said. "One guy said it was the single greatest experience of his life! He was holding Wanbli at the time and said that he had loved eagles since he was a little boy."

"Lots of people who wanted to pet bears or deer or beavers or even hold a hummingbird are so excited to be able to finally do it!" Hanna said. "I've heard lots of them say they've waited their whole lives for this."

"Huh," Avery smiled.

"Excuse me," someone said. "Do you work here?"

The four of them turned to see a young woman, with a baby on one hip and a toddler pulling at her hand.

"Can we help you?" Avery asked.

"Well, my son, here, wants to pet the 'big doggies'," the woman said, looking off to her right. "And I just wanted to check with you first."

Avery followed the woman's glance and saw three of the four big wolves sitting against the wall, tongues hanging out, obviously enjoying the activity around them. She smiled. "They would love it," she said. "The big one is Sugmanitu," she added.

The woman returned her smile and started toward the wolves.

"I think I'll go along," Jessie said, hurrying after and falling into step with the woman.

"And I can see someone trying to talk to Capa," Hanna said. "I'll just go and introduce them!" She hurried off toward the great beaver and the people who had stopped in front of him.

"I'll just take Wanbli back to his adoring public," Stuart said. "See you later!"

Avery waved and started toward the far corner of the room, where Phil and Igmu Taka still entertained.

"Ah, my sister," someone said.

Avery turned to see Seeking Eagle beside her, arms folded across his chest.

"Seeking Eagle!" she said. "Where have you been?"

"Oh, just taking care of some minor details," Seeking Eagle said, offhand.

Avery waved an arm. "Isn't this wonderful?"

He smiled and nodded. "It is." He, too looked around. "All is as it should be."

Avery looked at him. "You know, I've been thinking about what you said," she said. "That first time we met you."

Seeking Eagle frowned. "You mean about the great . . ."

"Great work, yeah," Avery said. "And I wondered if this might be it. Their Great Work."

Seeking Eagle let his eyes roam across the huge room once more. "They are certainly making a lot of people happy," he said.

"And helping people learn more about them," Avery said. "You should hear the comments!"

Seeking Eagle smiled. "Then perhaps this *is* their Great Work!" he said.

"Ha! I knew it!" Avery said.

"What gave it away?" Seeking Eagle asked. "The fact that the Great Spirit told us where to find gold? Or the fact that you five kids can talk to these animals? Or maybe that they came to life in the first place?"

Avery laughed. "I think . . . all of the above," she said. "When the magic water brought the spirits back to (what was left of) their bodies, their Great Work started." She frowned thoughtfully. "I know I have learned so much from them, just in the few weeks I've known them. Like, who knew that animals have a sense of humour?"

"You saw that in Mato almost immediately," Seeking Eagle said, smiling.

"And in the Sugmanitu crew shortly after that," Avery said.

Seeking Eagle laughed. "Oh, Sister, you must have heard of a wolf's sense of humour before now!"

"Nope. Never did," Avery said. "Most of the time, everyone is too scared of getting close to the business end of any animal to take much time to get to know them!"

Seeking Eagle smiled. "And now a new era is beginning," he said.

Avery smiled back. "A new era. I like that," she said. "And soon we will have our own building . . ."

"And you five members of the B.A.R.C. will be front and center."

Avery made a face. "I don't care about that!" she said. "Well, I do, a little. But only because I can help!"

Seeking Eagle smiled. "Of course," he said. Then suddenly, his smile disappeared. "But do not forget, my sister. There are other forces in this world. Forces that will try to undermine all you are doing here."

"Forces?" Avery turned and looked at him. "What do you mean?"

"I do not know," Seeking Eagle said. "I only repeat what the Spirit whispers." He looked at her. "But be prepared. You are these animals' keepers now. It is up to you to befriend, care for and protect them!"

"Don't worry, we will!" Avery said fiercely.

"Good." Seeking Eagle's smile was back. "Shall we go and . . . mingle?"

Avery smiled and followed him.

 Diane Stringam Tolley was born and raised on the great Alberta prairies. Daughter of a ranching family of writers, she inherited her love of writing at a very early age. Trained in Journalism, she has penned countless articles and short stories. She is the published author of five e-books and the Christmas novels, Carving Angels, (Kris Kringle's) Magic and SnowMan. She and her husband, Grant, live in Beaumont, Alberta, and are the parents of six children and grandparents of seventeen-plus.

She loves to hear from her readers...

Facebook : http://facebook.com/diane.tolley1

Twitter: http://twitter.com/StoryTolley

Web Site: www.dianestringamtolley.com

Blog: www.dlt-lifeontheranch.blogspot.com

Video: https://vimeo.com/45744176

Podcast: http://www.practicalpodcasting.com/kris-kringles-magic-diane-stringam-tolley-author/

 Megan Tolley is the eldest of Diane's grandchildren. Born with a love of books and reading, High Water is Megan's first written work.

49789196R00070

Made in the USA
Charleston, SC
04 December 2015